THE LUNATIC, THE SECRET SPORTSMAN AND THE WOMEN NEXT DOOR and VIBRATIONS

Stanley Eveling has rapidly made a name for himself as one of the most accomplished, varied and original new British dramatists. He combines a shrewd eye for observation with a professional understanding of the stage and brings to both a philosopher's ability to understand life and to draw conclusions from our behaviour. At the same time Mr. Eveling, who teaches moral philosophy at Edinburgh University, is very concerned with moral problems, and he imposes his ideas strongly on all his plays.

THE LUNATIC, THE SECRET SPORTSMAN AND THE WOMEN NEXT DOOR is a play that is broadly set in the tradition of absurdist drama, but its surrealism never detracts from the moral message and the approach of the author to extreme states of the mind, especially violence. First performed at Edinburgh's Traverse Theatre, it has never failed to fascinate its audience as well as often shocking a section of it. VIBRATIONS is a play about responsibility that in its brilliant dialogue and rapid movement of ideas never fails to hold the attention of the audience. Above all, Stanley Eveling is a writer's writer and his work is always a joy to read, coming alive from the printed page almost as effectively as from the stage.

By the same author:- Playscript 20, THE BALACHITES and THE STRANGE CASE OF MARTIN RICHTER and Playscript 37, COME AND BE KILLED and DEAR JANET ROSENBERG, DEAR MRS. KOONING.

PLAYSCRIPT 30

'the lunatic, the secret sportsman and the women next door' & 'vibrations'

stanley eveling

CALDER AND BOYARS · LONDON

First published in Great Britain 1970
by Calder and Boyars Limited
18 Brewer Street, London W1R 4AS

All performing rights in these plays
are strictly reserved and application
for performances should be made to
Harvey Unna Ltd,
Marylebone High Street, London W1

No performance of these plays may be
given unless a licence has been obtained
prior to rehearsal.

Printed in Great Britain by
The Pitman Press,
Bath, Somerset

CONTENTS

THE LUNATIC, THE SECRET SPORTSMAN
AND THE WOMEN NEXT DOOR

THE LUNATIC, THE SECRET SPORTSMAN AND THE WOMEN NEXT DOOR was first performed at the Traverse Theatre Club, Edinburgh in August 1968 with the following cast:

LUNATIC	Derick O'Connor
SPORTSMAN	Anthony Haygarth
ELSIE	Angela Galbraith
DORIS	Pamela Moiseiwitsch

The play was directed by Max Stafford-Clark.

SCENE ONE

(A room, containing, mainly, a bed to rear S.R. with
small table and small table lamp beside it, two doors,
one rear S.L., main entrance and exit, one S.R.
Mantlepiece rear centre with picture of school cricket
team. Picture of large forbidding woman on wall
married geometrically to a corresponding picture of
small, weak gentleman. Not much else, a table, bare,
and a few kitchen chairs, and a small trampoline, S.L.
Scene opens with stage empty, silent for a moment,
then the sound of drumming, growing louder, until
THE LUNATIC enters, finger drumming, goes round
and round the stage, pursued by the SECRET SPORTS-
MAN, dogging his footsteps. Round and round and
round they go. The noise is deafening, enough to drive
anybody mad. At last THE LUNATIC stops. So does
the SECRET SPORTSMAN. THE LUNATIC turns on the
SECRET SPORTSMAN.

LUNATIC. Stop following me around. There's no point in
it.

SPORTSMAN. (Ingratiatingly) Play some more.

LUNATIC. Push off.

SPORTSMAN. I admire you. I think you've got something
to say.

LUNATIC. Push off.

SPORTSMAN. Nobody else has, but you have. That drum...

(LUNATIC plays a tattoo)

9

SPORTSMAN. ... What's it for?

LUNATIC. Armageddon. Blood up to here. (Raises his
hands over his head)

SPORTSMAN. (Clambering up onto the trampoline. Does
small, tentative bounces, which can be larger if and
when he gets excited. He can also lie on it and peer
over the edge)

I thought so. Tell me about it.

LUNATIC. (Sits down on a chair) I used to be a painter.

SPORTSMAN. (Doing a few bounces) Oho...

LUNATIC. I painted a huge picture... eighty feet high.

SPORTSMAN. (A large bounce) Who of?

LUNATIC. Jesus Christ.

SPORTSMAN. Oh, him!

LUNATIC. A self-portrait.

SPORTSMAN. I'd love to see it. (Peers over the edge of
the trampoline) Was it cultural?

LUNATIC. It was too small. I painted another self-portrait
two hundred feet high.

SPORTSMAN. Was that good as well?

LUNATIC. The face was so far off the ground...

SPORTSMAN. (Bouncing, gently) Mmmm?

LUNATIC. ... I had to hang from the ceiling to see it. It
was a failure.

SPORTSMAN. (Stands on his hands, waves his legs in a
scissor movement) Altogether, how many pictures did
you paint? (Collapses)

10

LUNATIC. Not counting the early period, (He glances up at the two portraits) with its paintings of cows, sheep, goats, flies and flowers and my great religious period, I painted the following paintings...

(The SECRET SPORTSMAN begins a set of ·bounces)

... the Mona Lisa, the Bayswater Plastic Saint at her Ablutions, the Life and Crimes of George, Duke of Buckingham...

SPORTSMAN. Wheee...

LUNATIC. The Earl of Leicester, hunting, the Madonna and Child, all at a discount, and in oils, two hundred of the amatory acts of Leda and the Swan. Then I stopped.

SPORTSMAN. (Breathlessly) You'd done your best for the swine. I wish I could see them.

LUNATIC. They're all in galleries under a variety of assumed names. I didn't want the credit. (Pause) I'm going to sleep now.

SPORTSMAN. (Peers over the edge. Very pleased with everything) When you get there remember to come back where it's all happening.

LUNATIC. When my eyes are closed I'm asleep. (He closes his eyes) And inside here it's a red, fibrilled room of constant colour and size. And a huge woman is moving around me.

SPORTSMAN. Go on.

LUNATIC. She is about to perform an act of extreme obscenity. That's what I'm made of piss excrement and grey snot. I'm happy now. Be quiet.

SPORTSMAN. (Nods) Get on with it and when you come back we'll have a good laugh. (He begins a fine series of bounces) Normally, I'm more normal than this. Normally, I go in for refreshing, healthy exercises.

11

(Stops, lies on his back, feet in the air, peddles) I'm an expert boxer and I run over thirty miles a day. I take part in competitions. I could have been a champion. Every day I'm seen chatting to this person and that person... (He comes down, leans over and gazes warmly at THE LUNATIC) and no one guesses the fascination you have for me, you poor deranged creature... (He rolls over on his back, and rocks backwards and forwards) I know you're a nut-case but as soon as I hear you drumming I'm up here at the double and I can't leave you alone. (He stops rocking. Rolls onto his front, very young-boyish, puts his face between his hands and supports his body on his elbows, raises a rear leg occasionally) I suspect these feelings. (Sighs) They savour of the same kind I savoured at my favourite boarding school. The first time it happened I said 'Carruthers Minor, you're a filthy pig', and I punched his face in... (He gets into a Buddha position, legs crossed, bites his fingernails) ... but he just cried and cried and sat on my bed and we were chums ever after. (Falls back, does small bounces) So I developed a taste for it and I couldn't bear the sight of women. I've tried but it's no go... and yet I'm quite normal.

ELSIE. (Shouts from outside) Stop that fucking drumming.

SPORTSMAN. (Freezes. Sits up. Looks anxious) That's a woman.

ELSIE. Stop that fucking drumming.

SPORTSMAN. What an absolute bitch.

ELSIE. (Very angrily) Will you stop that fucking drumming.

SPORTSMAN. (Shouts) What?

ELSIE. Will you stop that fucking drumming.

SPORTSMAN. (Puts his fingers in his ears) What did you say?

ELSIE. Will you stop that fucking drumming.

SPORTSMAN. I can't hear what you say for this fucking drumming.

ELSIE. What?

SPORTSMAN. I can't hear what you say for this fucking drumming.

(ELSIE appears with hands over her hears. They stare at each other)

ELSIE. Stop that... (Takes her hands away) ... it's stopped.

SPORTSMAN. (Removes his fingers) Shh. He's asleep.

ELSIE. (Stares at him) It's you!

SPORTSMAN. Shhh. He's having a sleep.

ELSIE. Stupid, nasty, selfish pig. They should lock him away.

SPORTSMAN. What for?

ELSIE. He's a bad influence on you, Teddy.

SPORTSMAN. He's a good influence on me.

ELSIE. No, he isn't.

SPORTSMAN. I think so.

(He sits on the edge of the trampoline, dangling his legs over the side)

ELSIE. (Coyly) Why don't you ever come to see me nowadays? We've got a new piano.

SPORTSMAN. You won't let him bring his drum.

ELSIE. What does he want to bring his drum for when we've got a new piano.

13

SPORTSMAN. I don't know. That's what I'd like to find out.

ELSIE. We've got a new girl there, Teddy. Just for you, darling, she'll wear a school cap and little blue trousers and no knickers.

SPORTSMAN. (Wriggles) I'm not coming in any more. (Loftily) I may have to sit for Parliament after I've got some sense out of him. I may have to go to the people. But until that time I'm impotent.

ELSIE. If you sit for Parliament, love, you'll repeal all the anti-sex laws, won't you, darling, so that we girls can come out into the open and bring a little pleasure into people's lives.

SPORTSMAN. (Seriously) I don't know yet. Maybe 'yes', maybe 'no'. It all depends.

ELSIE. (Comes up to SECRET SPORTSMAN) Nasty, fat little piggy. (She tickles him)

SPORTSMAN. (Climbs up out of harm's reach) Stop it. Stop it. I'm warning you. What about this new girl?

ELSIE. (Goes over to mirror and begins to preen herself) Oh, you'll love her Teddy. She's from the North and very boyish. She's got no tits to speak of, and a nice, firm little stomach, and very firm buttocks, her bum, dear, and little hard hips. You and her put the boxing gloves on and I guarantee, absolutely guarantee, you'll have the biggest, best, most dazzling, super-duper whizz orgasm you've ever had.

SPORTSMAN. (Morosely) On the other hand I might impose Draconian laws. No sex between the hours of dawn and sunset and the nights to be kept pure and holy. No sport, except of a Spartan variety, young healthy boys, Hoplites, savage and beautiful, going into battle, hand in hand, the women weeping, bearing the children.

ELSIE. How do they manage that?

SPORTSMAN. Anyway, nothing's settled yet. I have to wait and see what he says.

ELSIE. He's got a hold over you.

SPORTSMAN. (Goes onto his head) I refuse to discuss it.

ELSIE. Come and kiss Mummy.

SPORTSMAN. Piss off.

ELSIE. (Sits herself down, makes herself comfortable) How's business?

SPORTSMAN. Pretty brisk. Two mergers, a take-over and a fly-over. We're showing an absolute profit of two thousand per cent, and the workers aren't suffering either. Our interests are identical.

ELSIE. You're a good man.

SPORTSMAN. (Comes down, onto his knees. Looks innocent and solemn) I've done my best according to my lights. (Turns to ELSIE) But one night, Elsie, I woke up, stared ahead and I spoke up. I said 'What's it all for?' I got no answer. Not a sound. The total comfort, the absolute success of my life, perished and crumbled; like candy floss at the first touch of hot spittal, Elsie. I got religion at first.

ELSIE. Very unctuously) Christ came to redeem sinners. Remember Mary Magdalen?

SPORTSMAN. Don't interrupt.

ELSIE. Ah, but he did, Teddy. I believe that and so do all my girls. They have to or out they go. I make sure they all have a bible beside their beds. It gives the place tone.

SPORTSMAN. I was telling you, Elsie, I got religion... I went straight to the top man, the Bishop in our local area, and I said, 'What's it all about, eh, Bishop?'

ELSIE. We had a Bishop visit my place once... he was absolutely wonderful. When he left he blessed all the girls and they all said he was a real man as well... which gives the lie...

SPORTSMAN. I got religion very badly indeed. I can't tell you how many pairs of trousers...

ELSIE. (Still pursuing her own thoughts) Oh, yes...

SPORTSMAN. Hundreds of pairs of trousers I wore out kneeling to the Lord God on his high silver throne. It's such a beautiful conception, Elsie. All the angels carrying those musical instruments. And what I read it definitely stated that we were the crown of creation.

ELSIE. Of course, I knew that from the first... there's weeds and plants and all that, above the dust, and next the reptiles and insects and then the sheep and the goats, not necessarily in that order, and then us, right at the top. And so it goes on, you can see that, right up to the very top. So it's all arranged, and even the low-liest will sit on the right hand. There's a place for everybody, yea, even unto the third and the fourth generation. I make all my girls repent every morning, just in case one of them's taken.

SPORTSMAN. But I saw through it, blast it; I just couldn't abide it after a bit; (He begins to clamber very care-fully from the trampoline) all those parsons and bishops and Popes were all talking absolute rubbish. Crash, just like a pack of cards. I walked out (He does a few knees bends to restore the circulation) and I've never been to a church service since that day.

(He sits down on THE LUNATIC's drum)

ELSIE. We'll have a lovely party the next time you're in. You can do what you like. Let it rip, Teddy, you can do exactly what you want. You'll be all the better for it.

SPORTSMAN. (Mournfully) I've got such horrible longings. You couldn't possibly cope with the horrible longings I've got.

LUNATIC. (Opens his eyes) I don't think I'm asleep any more.

ELSIE. Sod it. He's waking up.

SPORTSMAN. Go to hell.

ELSIE. Midnight, Teddy. We'll all be waiting for you.

SPORTSMAN. Piss off.

ELSIE. (Makes a mouth at him) Kiss, kiss. (Exits)

LUNATIC. You're sitting on my drum.

SPORTSMAN. I beg your pardon.

LUNATIC. It'll smell.

SPORTSMAN. I'm very sorry indeed.

LUNATIC. I dreamt a beautiful dream. Whoever sent that dream has my blessing.

SPORTSMAN. Do you have any news?

LUNATIC. I prophesy the end of all toil and labour; the end of all evolutionary items and that our biological equipment will become the sport of children; I prophesy ten centuries of continuous fun and laughter. (An hysterical announcement) Yea, yea!

SPORTSMAN. That's more like it.

LUNATIC. I'm exhausted. Now that I refuse all forms of nourishment the end can't be long.

SPORTSMAN. Don't die yet.

LUNATIC. I look forward to it. My brains are bleeding.

SPORTSMAN. Don't die until you've handed me the information I'm after. I worship the ground you walk on.

17

(He sits at THE LUNATIC's feet)

LUNATIC. (His head in his hands) I respect everything.
There s something to respect in a wicker-basket,
(He fingers the collar of the SECRET SPORTSMAN's
track suit) it's a great invention. The first spoon I
set eyes on I wept for joy. As for sunglasses (He
stares at the SECRET SPORTSMAN) that was worth
more gratitude than a lifetime of thankfulness.

SPORTSMAN. (Fervently) You're a blessed saint.

LUNATIC. (Raises his hands) It's evil where there's gaps.

SPORTSMAN. Drum, drum, drum. Oh, Christ, this is
lovely.

ELSIE. (Calls) Stop that. Will you stop that.

LUNATIC. I'm frightened.

SPORTSMAN. You're not.

LUNATIC. It's getting colder and colder.

ELSIE. (Off) Stop that! Will you stop that.

LUNATIC. Leave me alone, because it's got all electrical.
The sparks will fly. If you're an electrician, warn
everybody I'm alive. On the other hand, if you're an
atomic physicist, warn everybody again, inform them,
print some notices...

SPORTSMAN. What shall I say?

LUNATIC. Radio-active half-life, five and a half years.
Maximum security. Death after ten hours. Oh, I'm
exploding.

SPORTSMAN. Drum, drum, drum. Eh! What a character.

LUNATIC. Let them all know in time.

(Enter the women next door, ELSIE followed by DORIS

in her blue knockerbockers, etc.)

ELSIE. I've told you till I'm sick. If that lunatic doesn't stop his drumming I'm having him committed.

SPORTSMAN. Get out.

(ELSIE parades DORIS. DORIS is an incompetent amateur, new to the game, doing her best to distance herself from her real feelings)

ELSIE. Here's Doris. Now, what did I tell you.

SPORTSMAN. I can't be bothered with all that now.

ELSIE. (Looking at the LUNATIC who is now standing S.R. staring into space, blankly) He's off again. You'll not get a squeak out of him till I'm gone. I think he's frigid.

SPORTSMAN. Shhh. He's gone inactive.

ELSIE. This is Doris. What did I tell you?

DORIS. (Somewhat taken with THE LUNATIC) Is that him?

ELSIE. No, you stupid bitch. That's a lunatic.

DORIS. (Moves back) Ooh, I'm frightened of them.

ELSIE. You don't need to be frightened of him. He's just a bloody lunatic.

DORIS. I'm frightened of lunatics.

SPORTSMAN. Now, now, baby, you don't need to be frightened of that gentleman. He's not dangerous. Not dangerous in the least. In fact, my little treasure, he's quite harmless.

DORIS. I'm scared of lunatics. We had one in our street, you know, he was simple. He used to chase all the girls and try to grab them. He never grabbed me. I'd have died.

19

SPORTSMAN. Oh, pet. She's lovely, Elsie. All you said and more. I can't wait.

ELSIE. What did I say, Teddy. Isn't she a beauty? Isn't she just?

SPORTSMAN. You bloody old lesbian.

DORIS. Is this the one then?

SPORTSMAN. I love those little knockerbockers.

DORIS. Wouldn't you like to see Doris in a pretty little dress?

SPORTSMAN. You're sweet as you are. And don't call yourself Doris. It doesn't suit you.

DORIS. Whatever you say, pet. What's my name, then?

SPORTSMAN. You're my chum, Carruthers Minor. I call you Billy.

DORIS. (Disconcerted, embarrassed) Christ! I'm a boy, then. O.K. We'll have some spiffing good fun.

SPORTSMAN. When we fight we won't really hurt each other, Billy.

ELSIE. I'll leave you two boys together. Bye bye, now.

SPORTSMAN. Say 'bye bye' to Mummy, Billy.

(ELSIE exits)

DORIS. (Disgusted) Jesus!

SPORTSMAN. You rotter. Who taught you to swear?

DORIS. Hey, Teddy, are you sure that loony's alright?

SPORTSMAN. Of course he is.

DORIS. Why's his eyes open, then?

20

SPORTSMAN. He's far away.

DORIS. Does he talk?

SPORTSMAN. He mostly plays his drum.

DORIS. Why does he do that?

SPORTSMAN. I don't know.

DORIS. He's spooky.

SPORTSMAN. Spooky, spooky, spooky. You're yellow, Billy.

DORIS. He's just staring at us.

(She is walking round him, inspecting him)

SPORTSMAN. Let's play something.

(DORIS shrugs her shoulders. Makes a face at THE LUNATIC, turns on her heels)

DORIS. Okay.

SPORTSMAN. Let's play ring a ring a roses.

DORIS. (Amused) That's a girl's game.

SPORTSMAN. When we grow up, Billy, we'll have to know all about girls.

DORIS. (Ironically) We hate girls, eh, Teddy?

SPORTSMAN. Yes. Girls are soft.

DORIS. What's that badge?

(She points to a badge on the SECRET SPORTSMAN's track suit)

SPORTSMAN. (Looks down at it) I'm a rotarian.

DORIS. Oh, I've heard of that. You must be very important.

SPORTSMAN. That's nothing. Play along with me, baby, and you'll be alright. I'm a freemason, a wykamist, a member of the Free Council of Churches; I also believe in Moral Rearmament, or we're finished. I've got shares in the Lord's Day Observance Society and I'm one of the few people to have actually signed the Potsdam agreement.

DORIS. (Impressed) You must be very clever. I'm not clever like that. I never signed that Potsdam agreement. We used to sign things at the door. And we had visits from the Salvation Army, of course.

SPORTSMAN. (Loftily) That's not the same thing. That's for poor people.

DORIS. (Involved) We were very poor people. We were fumigated. My Dad died in his early forties. He was a real brute. Always going on about the government. My mother used to say if the men would only do what they were told the government would help them.

SPORTSMAN. I've got a lot of decisions to make, Doris. I might go into politics. I've made my packet. I could retire tomorrow. But all those memberships are useless if I don't know what it's all for.

DORIS. That's what Dad used to say. (She sighs) He used to say, what's it all for? My mother'd say there must be a meaning to it. It used to make him mad.

(The SECRET SPORTSMAN has been looking at THE LUNATIC with some satisfaction)

SPORTSMAN. He's a marvellous man.

DORiS. What's that, love?

SPORTSMAN. Call me Teddy.

DORIS. Teddy.

22

SPORTSMAN. Him. The lunatic.

DORIS. He makes me sweat all over. He does, Teddy. He gives me the shivers.

SPORTSMAN. He's not young, you know.

DORIS. Isn't he?

SPORTSMAN. You can tell by the wrinkles and the white hair. No, he's getting on a bit.

DORIS. That's his drum, isn't it?

SPORTSMAN. When I first met him he had a full head of hair, chestnut coloured. He was quite pretty. But after he'd been living with me for a bit he began to show his real age. His hair went white and then he got those wrinkles.

DORIS. He's got a lovely mouth. That's a funny thing.

SPORTSMAN. Oh, yes, he'd hardly been with me for six months before he'd gone completely white. When I first saw him he had lovely chestnut curls. He looked about twenty. Like an angel from Eton. He was lost. He looked as if he'd been crying. I took him in. He was a lunatic. He came like a lamb. 'What would you like?' I said - sit on my knee, Billy - and at first he didn't answer - there, there, little dimpled knees - so I kept on at him, I wouldn't let him sleep; he likes to go off and sleep, like he is now - sweet little knees... and what's that I see - 'No, no, no', I said 'no sleepy bye byes till you've told your best friend Teddy what it is you want; no sleep for you'. I left the light on and I played gramophone records...

DORIS. Ooooh, he's funny. Just staring at us. What a funny man he is. Hello...

SPORTSMAN. Little buttons, little buttons - so he didn't get to sleep and one day, it was a Thursday, no, I lie, a Friday it was, I'll never forget it, he broke. He said - I hate girls, don't you Billy, they're so pretentious?

- drum, drum, drum, he said. And that was that.

DORIS. What a lovely story.

SPORTSMAN. We'll switch off the lights, eh, Bill? We'll
have some secret sports. I fought most of the second
world war in the dark. We were against Hitler, of
course, but who's to say he wasn't right after all. He
was a bulwark against Communism and I notice quite a
few people are taking the Hitler line nowadays but they
don't give him the credit. Give a dog a bad name... so,
just switch the light off and we'll have a little sleep.
We'll talk a bit and fight a bit and matron'll come round
soon now, so we'd better not make too much noise.

DORIS. Oh, Teddy... I don't want to switch the lights off.

SPORTSMAN. Switch them off.

DORIS. But think of him, glinting in the star light, Teddy.
Terrible. Ghosts look like him, Teddy, ghouls and war-
locks, and Princes of Darkness and fairies that come
and take bad girls away. Isn't that soft? But it's the
sort of thing that just pops into your head when you're
not thinking.

SPORTSMAN. Switch the light off.

DORIS. Will he move?

SPORTSMAN. I've told you. He's switched off. He's not
working.

DORIS. You switch it off.

SPORTSMAN. Oh, alright. But I'll have something to say
to that old bitch when I see her. You don't seem to know
what you're supposed to do, Doris whatever your name
is.

DORIS. I'm sorry, Teddy. It's just him. Couldn't you tell
him to go?

SPORTSMAN. No, no. He's as deaf as a post.

24

DORIS. (Amazed) Is he?

SPORTSMAN. For Christ's sake. Of course he is. And blind.

DORIS. (Shocked) Oh, no!

SPORTSMAN. I'm telling you. Deaf and blind. He had an accident. He lost the use of his eyes. He had the sight burnt out of them. And he went deaf as well. That's why he's drumming all the time.

DORIS. Oh, I wondered.

SPORTSMAN. You're really stupid, Billy. He's able to go on drumming because he's deaf. That's the benefit he gets from lacking that faculty.

DORIS. All the same...

SPORTSMAN. Don't touch him, that's all.

DORIS. Why?

SPORTSMAN. Don't touch him. Say no more.

DORIS. You switch the light off then. I might bump into him.

SPORTSMAN. Shit. Alright. The bed's over there.

DORIS. Shall I keep my knockerbockers on?

SPORTSMAN. Bad boy. Course you do. Teddy'll have to take his pants off but Billy can wear his little buttoned knockerbockers in bed.

(DORIS hops into bed, stares soulfully out, with sheets up to her neck)

SPORTSMAN. Are you comfy?

DORIS. Super.

SPORTSMAN. Right.

(He goes over to the switch and switches it off)

DORIS. Ooooh, it's dark.

SPORTSMAN. I've switched the light off.

DORIS. It's dark without the light.

SPORTSMAN. Don't talk. I've got to be careful.

(He makes his way very carefully towards the bed)

I don't want to bump into him.

DORIS. What'll he do?

SPORTSMAN. (Irritably) Whoops. Phew. That was the
table. Are you there?

DORIS. (Whispers) Yes. Come on. These sheets are cold.

SECRET SPORTSMAN. (Sighs with relief) There we are.

(The bed creaks beneath his bulk)

You face the wall, Billy... that's nice.

(Sounds of SECRET SPORTSMAN snuggling down.
Grunts)

Nice, nice, nice. I say, Bill, did I tell you, they've
picked me for the first team, on the wing, I'm playing
on the wing, sweetie, on the wing, sweetie...

DORIS. Oh, Teddy, you fat little bugger... Oh...

(Pause)

LUNATIC. I'm alone here in the vast hall and the King and
Queen are laying a tomb on the wreath of the unknown
shoulder. Cats like cream. And the great cathedral
reverberates with the sound of a million voices and bells

ring from every steeple. But not on their whiskers.
It's a national occasion. He died that we might live.
They shall not grow cold as we that are left grow cold,
nor wages freeze them nor their tears pretend. At
Vimy, Passendale, at Waterloo and King's Cross,
they commute the night's long thunder; though many are
cold but few are frozen. They chopped off his head.
I'm standing in a huge car park and I want to say, here
and now, if love is the answer, what was the question,
good Gertrude, don't. Because inside we're all pink,
like Queen Victoria, so who's to say that niggers
aren't human. I blessed a cow for bearing a horn which
blew and the forest rang. God bless the Prime Minister,
the President and the Rules of the Game. Most people
can't stand each other. Lunatics can't think. But that's
no answer. Scramble the brains of a telephone and
pick up the receiver. Hello lover, why don't you
answer? But at the end of a wire your dead boy-friend
is trying to get a word in edgeways. Mother goodbye.
The baby's alive and kicking. The pail's fallen over.
Somebody is wicked. What of that? Somebody blew off
my ears. What of that as well? Somebody put a sizzling
poker through each eye-ball. There are hundreds like
us. So why does everybody stare like that? I'm quite
normal. It's better to wake up with a clear head. Lord
Montgomery has flung a right jaw at the boot of the
axis. So they marched. What the Queen actually said
was, in parenthesis, I'm a German myself. But the
skins of the Jews hung at the window panes say, in
German, 'Patriotic'. That's my theory. Anyway, Adam
shouldn't've eaten the whole apple and then screwed
Eve. In the Gardens of Allah you'll find just as good
Christians as any as go to church every Sunday. Who's
to blame them? I saw in the last circle a Soul whose
face was wonderful and I said, more in sorrow than in
anger, why are you so solemn, and he was so much a
gentleman he didn't even notice my presence. The
dragon was curled round hiw bowels and his smoke
puffs out at the lips of Vesusvius. I admire Ulysses.
He was a cunning traveller. But the Gorgon also
deserves some sympathy. Drum, drum, drum.

(ELSIE opens the door, tip-toes in)

ELSIE. Hello. Hello, there. Are you sleepers? Are the love-boys sleepers? It's all darky in here. Shall Mummy switch on the lights?

SPORTSMAN. Shhh. We're asleep.

ELSIE. Ha, ha. Who's that naughty boy talking? I'm coming to see you. I'm coming... aaaaaaaaah...

(ELSIE gives a startled shriek. We hear sounds of a struggle, a sort of whine from the LUNATIC, a gurgle from ELSIE, and a cry of...)

ELSIE. For Christ's sake!

SPORTSMAN. Blast and bugger.

(The bed creaks. The SECRET SPORTSMAN gets up very quickly. We hear the sound of a stick, a fist or some heavy object striking something repeatedly. DORIS is shrieking. It's pandemonium)

SPORTSMAN. Switch the bloody light on. Switch it on. Switch it on.

(DORIS switches on the light. THE LUNATIC is standing, rather bloodstained. With his eyes open. The SECRET SPORTSMAN, in vest and underpants, is standing in front of him with his stick, fist or heavy object raised. The woman next door is lying on the ground. DORIS is standing by the light switch, with one hand on the switch and the other holding up her knickerbockers so that the flies are kept closed. End of scene)

SCENE TWO

(The same, exactly, all frozen in exactly the same positions, for a second)

SPORTSMAN. I thought she'd bugger it all up.

DORIS. What about him?

SPORTSMAN. Bugger it all up. Aaaaaah. I could spit. If this leaks out I'm done for.

DORIS. He should be locked up.

SPORTSMAN. Damn and blast it all. This is going to ruin my career.

(He sits down, head in hands. DORIS begins to adjust her clothing in a decent and seemly manner)

DORIS. What about her?

SPORTSMAN. What a scandal. Prominent city figure caught in compromising posture. My God, the headlines.

DORIS. Vehemently) What do we do about her?

SPORTSMAN. What're you jabbering about?

DORIS. Her. On the floor. Shouldn't we do something about it?

SPORTSMAN. What? Bury her, you mean? Come to think of it...

DORIS. What d'you mean, bury her? She's not dead.

SPORTSMAN. Dead! Of course she's dead. Once he gets his fingers on you it's curtains.

DORIS. (Hesitates towards ELSIE, looks down at her) She's not dead.

SPORTSMAN. She is dead. Look at her. She'll start to smell in a minute.

DORIS. What're we going to do?

SPORTSMAN. You may well ask. That is a question you might very well put to yourself. One thing's certain, she's not lying in state in my residence.

DORIS. What're we going to do?

(She is near to tears)

SPORTSMAN. Quack, quack, quack. Give me a hand.

DORIS. What're we...?

SPORTSMAN. Give me a hand. (He tries to lift her) You great bag of guts. Horrible fat creature. It's a merci-ful release.

DORIS. Where are you taking her?

SPORTSMAN. You stay here. In case anybody comes.

(He begins to drag her out)

Say I'm engaged. It's a good job I'm in shape. Try to think of something.

DORIS. (Panic-stricken) Don't leave me here with this... Teddy... Teddy...

(Exits SECRET SPORTSMAN. She looks apprehensively at THE LUNATIC who looks at nothing. She goes round him. She climbs onto the bed. She spits at him)

DORIS. Homicide. Bloody murderer. I've seen faces like
yours. In the Sunday newspapers. Homicidal maniac.
That's what you're called. That's you. Beast. Rotten
sod. You'll get us all in trouble. Blind, as well. You
couldn't be more spooky.

(She gets more courageous and the reminder that he is
blind awakens some feelings in her. She gets up. Circles
round him)

You can't hear what I'm saying either, can you? It
must be awful. No wonder you're bonkers. It's no
wonder. Fancy killing a poor old woman like that
though... that was naughty, you know. It really was.
Just for touching you. People have to be touched, you
know. Did you not know that? Mind you, ·I'm not saying
I don't agree with you. There's far too much touching
going on. There I agree with you. Far too much...

(Pause)

Do you have a name, pet? Oh, I forgot... I tell you
what, I'll call you Tinker. I used to have a dog called
Tinker. I really did. He got run over of course. Oh, it
was awful. Poor old Tinker. He'd got blood all over
him... Somebody should clean you up... But how can
they, you bloody loony, when you won't let anybody
touch you? You're touched... (She giggles) that's
what it is; so you'll just have to stand there with all
that blood all over you. What gets me is you don't show
any signs of consternation whatsoever, not a bloody
sign. (She stares hard at him) That Teddy's a real
savage. He is, you know. You get to know them. When
you've been fingered as much as I have... you get to
know them. He's the sort. Do you know, there's some
of them, they tear at your clothes just like you were a
parcel. I know what it's like being touched. Girls get
touched all the time. They call it feeling you up.
Christ... You look a bit like my dad. Honest. I used
to sit on his knees. That was alright really. Though
mind you, I bet he was getting a bit of a stand on.
Hmmmm. What an awful thing to say. It's funny though,
I feel I can talk to you. It's like talking to a dummy.
Except you can talk... I wanted all the nice things,

31

really, I wanted, oh, you know... all the nice things...
I wanted a bit of fun. There's not much fun around, is
there? I ask you... You may well be wondering how I
got myself into all this, well, you know what I mean.
Well, you see, (She sits herself on the table beside
where he is standing) I meet this boy at this dance and,
you know, he's alright, he's got a lovely way with him,
some of them have, and anyway I was fed up at home...
Doris do this, Doris, do that, Doris is my real name,
you know, well, anyway, so when he said he'd got this
car, I thought to myself, right, so off we went and...
and... here I am. (She bursts into tears. She cries
and then blinks her eyes, shakes her head) Do you
have a... oh, no, I forgot. Never mind. You must
think I'm awful, going on like this. It just came over
me. You don't know you're lonely until you find somebody to listen to you... then you know you're lonely.
Ah, well. It's not so bad. Hmmm. (Pause. She smiles)
You must think I'm really selfish. I am, I suppose. I
just got fed up, nothing was good enough for our Doris
so I thought, right, it's your turn now, Doris, and
anyway... and anyway... (She bursts into tears again,
speaks through her sobs) It was awful what you did, it
really was, killing that poor old woman, that was a
terrible thing to do... you frightened me, you did...
why can't you talk... you bloody loony... you... no...
I don't know what I'm saying... you can't help it. I
don't think I'll call you Tinker after all. No. (She
comes close to him) You're not bad looking. D'you
know that? You're not. If you had a nice shirt on and
that, you'd be really dishy. That white hair suits you,
because your face is quite young, really. That horrible
Teddy doesn't know a thing he's talking about. He's
well-known, though. She was telling me before we
came in, if you play your cards right, he's... he's...
What're you looking at?... Do you know, Tinker, if
you'd been the one, not that horrible Teddy, did you
see how he went on, that's horrible, really, making me
wear these silly things. I'm not bad looking myself,
though I do say so, you should see me with my glad rags
on... I wish you'd let me touch you... will you?...
Will you let Doris just touch you... (She puts out a
timorous paw) on the sleeve... eeh, I'm frightened...

I want to touch you, you've got such a lovely mouth, all
soft and juicy and red... and lovely eyes. I bet your
skin's as soft as a baby's... I bet; and I bet those hands
of yours, Teddy said they were very strong; won't you
let Doris touch you, just a little bit...? You're nasty,
d'you know that, you've got to let people touch you, get
really warm and close, touching, touching, touching,
it's so... nice, it really is; come on. Eh? I tell you
what, I'll go and change, I'll go and put some clothes
on. Well, you know what I mean. I'll put on my best
dress and some stockings and my best shoes and then
you'll see. And listen, Tinker, I won't blame you at
all. And if you want to do that to me I won't be angry
... Oh, Christ, I feel awful... Now, you stay there,
Tinker, will you now? I'm no good to anybody... I'll
put on a nice dress and I'll come and wash all that
blood off. I don't care. So there... Bye... Tinker.

(She leaves. THE LUNATIC stands there. He stares
ahead. He lifts his hand, feels his face. He smiles. He
feels in his pocket, finds a half-smoked cigarette, puts
it to his lips. Takes out a box of matches. Lights the
cigarette. Inhales. Blows out smoke. Looks around for
somewhere to put the ash. Sees nothing. Puts his hands
to his face again. Sees a mirror, looks at his face in
it. Fingers his face)

LUNATIC. What a sight!

(Exits, smoking)

(Enter DORIS, all tarted up, wearing a hat)

DORIS. Tinker... there, what d'you think of... that...
Tinker... Where are you?... hiding? Tinker...
where are you? Bloody men.

(Exit DORIS)

(Enter SECRET SPORTSMAN dressed as ELSIE. He
makes a dramatic entrance, showing himself)

SPORTSMAN. Tra-la. (Looks around. Sniffs) Smoke?
Doris... hello... (Goes over to the bed, looks

around) He's left his bloody drum. Doris. Where is
the bitch? Jesus.

(Exits in consternation)

(Enter ELSIE, very painfully, breathes very harshly.
Dressed as the SECRET SPORTSMAN)

ELSIE. Teddy. What d'you think you're doing, Teddy? I'm
black and blue. (She sees herself in mirror) Oh, my
God. What a sight I look. The fat fool. What does he
think he's doing? Where are they all? Where's that
bloody lunatic? My God. The things I go through, all
for that ungrateful Teddy. He's gone mad. What a sight
I look. My God.

(Exit ELSIE)

(Enter LUNATIC. He looks around. Sees his drum.
Picks it up, slips cord round his neck. Switches off
main light. Exits drumming)

(Enter SECRET SPORTSMAN. He stumbles over something. Goes over to the bed, switches on bedside lamp)

SPORTSMAN. I'm bloody exhausted. Where's that bloody
lunatic? He's forgotten his drum... no, he hasn't...
it's gone. They've all gone. I'm absolutely whacked.
Not as fit as I used to be. My God. (He collapses on
the bed) Ouch. These bloody suspenders. Every time
I bend over the blood rushes out of my legs. (He
loosens them) Ah, that's better.

(Enter DORIS)

DORIS. Tinker, are you there, love? Tinker. Look at
Doris.

(He sees the SECRET SPORTSMAN, takes him for
ELSIE. She gives a shriek. The SECRET SPORTSMAN
sits bolt upright)

SPORTSMAN. What... what... oh, it's you.

34

(DORIS stares at him, flabberghasted)

SPORTSMAN. Well?

DORIS. You gave me a fright. What're you dressed up like
that for? You look a real sight.

SPORTSMAN. Shhh. Come in and shut the door. (He gets
up) I don't know how you girls manage. These stays
are cutting my ribs to pieces.

DORIS. What sort of game is this?

SPORTSMAN. Mind you, Doris, apart from that, (He sits
down, adjusts his clothing) they're not so bad. It's a
funny sensation, like walking about inside a woman. I
can't honestly say it's unpleasant.

DORIS. You're a queer old bugger and no mistake.

SPORTSMAN. Don't say that. I've got references from the
highest in the land. No, no, it takes a bit of getting
used to and I'll have to let this waist out a bit but I'll
soon get used to it.

DORIS. How do you mean?

SPORTSMAN. Don't you see? Can't you grasp it? It'll stay
on as her till the fuss dies down.

DORIS. What fuss?

SPORTSMAN. No, what I mean is I'll be her and nobody'll
know the difference.

DORIS. Won't they?

SPORTSMAN. Not in a bad light. We'll carry on the
business just as normal. Then, after a bit, I'll announce
I'm off on a world cruise and that'll be that.

DORIS. It'll never work.

SPORTSMAN. What worries me is that lunatic. You'll

have to go out and find him, Doris.

DORIS. Not me. Catch me going round the streets looking
for a lunatic with a drum. You can fry in your own
juice for all I care.

SPORTSMAN. (Sighs. Gets up. Preens in the mirror) Ah,
well, it's understandable. (Smiles at DORIS) What
worries me is he mightn't come, not seeing me like
this; it might have a bad effect on him.

DORIS. Eh?

SPORTSMAN. (Returns to preen) Still, it's not a bad idea.
It'll give me a chance to get used to these clothes. Oho.
You know, Doris, it could be a blessing in disguise.
She's got a nice little business here, it's the best of
both worlds really, we girls can have a high old time
when you're not on duty and meantime it's more relax-
ing being a woman I think. There's not the strain
involved. Do you think this pink suits me?

DORIS. God knows what you look like.

SPORTSMAN. You're just jealous.

DORIS. Me?

SPORTSMAN. Course you are. Anyway, we'll have a nice
chat and a cup of tea later and then we'll get down to
business. We'll have to get rid of the body, of course.
We can't have that stinking the place out. Meantime,
lovey, I'm off to get that lunatic. Men. You can't trust
them an inch. Whoops.

(Kicks up his legs and exits)

DORIS. (Shouts after him) You look like a transvestite
monkey... I wish I was back in Bradford. Oh, dear.

(ELSIE enters, dressed as the SECRET SPORTSMAN)

ELSIE. When I get hold of that Secret Sportsman I'll cut off
his balls.

36

DORIS. (Taking ELSIE for the SECRET SPORTSMAN) Oh, thank God. You've got yourself back in your own clothes again.

ELSIE. (Peers) Who's that? Doris?

DORIS. Who d'you... oh, my God, it's you. Oh, no... no, no... you're not wearing his clothes, are you?... are you?... I thought you were dead... you're not dead, are you?... are you...?

(She is somewhat hysterical and laughing, losing control of herself)

ELSIE. (Slaps her face) Control yourself. What's the matter with you? Are you having a nervous breakdown or something.

DORIS. Leave me alone.

ELSIE. That bloody loony. My body's black and blue. Have you seen Teddy?

DORIS. He's gone off dressed up as you to look for the lunatic.

ELSIE. That Teddy. Sometimes I think he's not right in his mind. Oh, my bones.

(She totters to a seat)

DORIS. What've you got his clothes on for?

ELSIE. I don't know. It's that Teddy. One of his bloody jokes. I'll give him bloody jokes. I'll expose him for the monster he is. It takes all sorts to make a world but he's something extra. He's a blot. That's what he is. Him and his bloody lunatic.

DORIS. (Miserably) I want to go home.

ELSIE. (Swiftly practical again) Don't be soft. You'll be throwing away a good career. You've got real ability and I wouldn't say that to everybody. You've got a definite flair.

DORIS. Thanks very much.

ELSIE. Anyway, they're not all like Teddy, you know.
Some of them behave like Christians and gentlemen.
Did I ever tell you about J.H. Crabtree?

DORIS. (Wearily) No. (Takes her shoes off)

ELSIE. Don't take your shoes off.

DORIS. Why not? My feet are killing me.

ELSIE. My God. What selfishness! I've just been beaten
black and blue by an expert. It's that drumming. He's
got muscles in his finger tips... Mind you, (Muses)
till I started to go I quite... ah, well, he must have
been a bonny man... what was I talking about?

DORIS. I don't know...

ELSIE. J.H. Crabtree.

DORIS. Mmmm...

ELSIE. Mr. J.H. Crabtree. A real Christian and a
Gentleman. Do you know, Doris, I warm to the thought
of him; do you know, before he entered one of the girls
he would always wash his hands and say 'May I
intrude?' That's courtesy for you. J.H. Crabtree.
Hmmm. Happy times, happy times.

DORIS. I don't give a damn about J.H. Thingamajig. I just
want to scream.

ELSIE. That's right, dear. You have a good scream. Get
it all out of your system. You know, I was just thinking,
when we've got rid of those two, Teddy and that lunatic
of his, you and me, we might just shut up shop and get
off for a holiday. I've got a good bit put by, what with
one thing and another. You know, Doris, I've not had
a holiday, not a real holiday, for I just don't know how
long it'll be. We might go on a world cruise.

DORIS. A world cruise. (She screams)

ELSIE. (Calmly) Why not. You're only young once. All
those lovely places, Fiji, Tonga, Basutoland, New
Zealand... we wouldn't lack for companionship. I've
seen it on the films, lonely widow and her beautiful
young daughter. We'll have a high old time.

DORIS. Oh, I don't know.

ELSIE. Yes, you do. You'll jump at the chance. I've quite
taken a fancy to you. You know what I mean?

DORIS. No, I don't know what you mean.

ELSIE. Well, I don't mean what you think I mean.

DORIS. Oh.

ELSIE. The very idea. Come and give Mummy a big kiss.

DORIS. What!

ELSIE. (Goes over to DORIS. Puts her arms around her.
Kisses her cheek) There, there. You shouldn't get
yourself so upset about things, dear. I mean, I know
it doesn't happen in Bradford but that's only because
they've got all their skeletons very firmly locked up in
their cupboards up there. What you've seen here today,
with Teddy and that, it's quite normal and the sooner
you wake up to that fact the better. (She fondles
DORIS's hair) The sooner you get that pretty little
nose rubbed in it the better you'll be. (Somehow
DORIS finds herself sitting on ELSIE's knee) There's
people at this moment going through far worse things.
Teddy's a fool but there's lots like him. He means well
and he's got big problems. Make no mistake about that.
As for that lunatic, well, he's a trouble-maker and
there's plenty of them around.

DORIS. (Weakly) I don't think he's half as bad as that
Teddy.

ELSIE. Teddy wouldn't harm a fly. Oh, he's not a man, of

course, but how many of them do you find around
nowadays. All his power goes to getting on in the world.
When he gets home he likes to relax.

DORIS. Teddy lives here?

ELSIE. Well, he calls it his peedatear, somewhere to take
his boots off, he says.

DORIS. All the same you're not telling me that what's going
on here is normal.

ELSIE. Normal, normal. You Northern girls make me sick.
Down here everything's normal. You've got to learn to
cope.

DORIS. I don't think I want to.

ELSIE. Oh, you don't, don't you.Well, that's up to you. Go
back to Bradford, if you want to, or whatever it's
called, but there's just as many places in Bradford to
get yourself into a right mess in as any you'll find down
here. However, Doris, I'm only speaking for your own
good. D'you understand.

DORIS. Yes.

ELSIE. That's the way. There. (She gives DORIS a
squeeze) You and me'll have a lovely world cruise,
see if we don't. (Briskly) Now, I want you to go and
put a face on and get yourself out and grab hold of that
Teddy, get him back here with my garments and if he
won't come tell him I'll have his balls off if he doesn't.
Okay?

DORIS. (Getting up) Okay.

ELSIE. (Pats her posterior) That's a good girl. Remember
what I said. It's not all my girls I'd take the same
trouble over, so mind yourself.

DORIS. Okay. I get the message.

ELSIE. Good girl... good girl...

(DORIS leaves)

ELSIE. Idiot! Not an idea in her head...! Thank God...!
Normal, the very idea!

(Enter LUNATIC. Looks around. Sees ELSIE whom he
supposes to be the SECRET SPORTSMAN)

LUNATIC. It's cold outside. Cold. There'll be snow.
There'll be...

ELSIE. Oh, it's you is it... what're you staring at?

LUNATIC. You...

ELSIE. You can talk, then. That's a blessing. And you
can see. Well, look at these bruises.

(The LUNATIC fumbles in his pockets. Takes out a
pair of scissors. Examines them)

ELSIE. Here, now...

(The LUNATIC smiles, shakes his head. Fumbles in
his pocket. Takes out a yoyo. Plays with it)

ELSIE. You make me sick.

(The LUNATIC puts the yoyo away. Takes out a bar of
chocolate. Holds it out to ELSIE)

ELSIE. What have you got there... eh... what is it?

(He smiles and nods)

ELSIE. What do you take me for, eh?... I'm not coming
near you ... not bloody likely. What's up with you, cat
got your tongue?

LUNATIC. It's... chocolate.

ELSIE. Is it?

LUNATIC. It's... milk chocolate.

41

ELSIE. Teddy's out looking for you.

LUNATIC. Ladies like chocolate.

ELSIE. It's no good you putting on that act with me. You're a thoroughly bad lot.

LUNATIC. You take...

ELSIE. Not me. God knows how long that thing's been in your pocket.

LUNATIC. Chocolate.

ELSIE. Oh God! Me... no... want... lunatic's choccy... savvy?

LUNATIC. You like... Very sweet... for lady.

ELSIE. Christ... no... thank... you. Teddy-master. You find... pretty damn quick.

LUNATIC. Me sorry, hurt poor fat lady.

ELSIE. Bloody cheek...

LUNATIC. You take, eat, have good time.

ELSIE. (Desperately) I've told you, I don't want it.

LUNATIC. You eat, swallow, yum, yum.

ELSIE. Oh God... where's that Teddy? Thank you... very... much. There's no need to bother...

LUNATIC. Bother...!

(He makes a step towards her)

ELSIE. Oh... me not angry... understand... me, Elsie, lovely forgiving nature...

LUNATIC. You good fat lady. You want chocolate. Good for you.

ELSIE. (Patience exhausted) Piss off.

LUNATIC. Look. I eat. See. Good.

ELSIE. That's right, dear. You have a good feed and then go and look for Teddy.

LUNATIC. You Teddy.

ELSIE. Eh?

LUNATIC. You Secret Sportsman.

ELSIE. No, no. Me woman next door.

LUNATIC. Woman next door old fat cow. Teddy know. Teddy say, old fat cow next door been screwed by a donkey. Take on anything... free.

ELSIE. When I see that Teddy... That's horrible. Horrible. You shouldn't believe all you hear. It's all lies.

LUNATIC. Why you wear funny clothes? You lunatic or something?

ELSIE. How d'you mean?

LUNATIC. You eat or pretty damn quick lunatic go off his head. No knowing what disasters will follow. Compris?

ELSIE. Don't come near me.

LUNATIC. Eat, fat creature.

ELSIE. Oh, alright. Give's a bit.

LUNATIC. Good. In my country men love fat ladies. Fat ladies not move. Stay in hut. Have babies. Sons. Good.

ELSIE. Oho. Very nice, I'm sure.

LUNATIC. Lunatic's tribe not believe in white medicine. Babies good, birth pills bad.

ELSIE. Oh, yes.

LUNATIC. Soon all white women all pills, no babies, all black women all babies, no pills. Soon all black, no white, God help us. Highly satisfactory.

ELSIE. You've got a point there, dearie.

LUNATIC. Me go now.

ELSIE. Good.

LUNATIC. Not good. Bad. You say, try say 'bad'.

ELSIE. Bad.

LUNATIC. Good.

ELSIE. Good.

LUNATIC. What?

ELSIE. Good.

LUNATIC. What?

ELSIE. Oh, Christ!

LUNATIC. Blasphemer.

ELSIE. Sometimes I think you're not as cracked as you make out. You're sly.

LUNATIC. Atheist.

ELSIE. Not at all, not at all. As I said to Teddy, I've always taken a strong religious line.

LUNATIC. Your face...

ELSIE. What?

LUNATIC. It's all covered with chocolate.

ELSIE. Oh!

LUNATIC. Let me wipe it off.

ELSIE. No, no, thank you kindly.

LUNATIC. Please.

ELSIE. Lord help us.

(The LUNATIC takes out a handkerchief, moistens it in his mouth and cleans ELSIE's face)

LUNATIC. There we are. It wasn't so bad, was it?

ELSIE. I don't get you at all. I really don't.

LUNATIC. I'm cold.

ELSIE. Yes, it is a bit chilly. That Teddy. All his millions and he won't have a fire.

LUNATIC. I'm freezing.

ELSIE. What you need is a cup of tea.

LUNATIC. Tea...

ELSIE. Yes, tea, brown liquid made in a pot...

LUNATIC. Tea?

ELSIE. Yes, tea. Tea. Oh, never mind.

LUNATIC. You'd like some tea?

ELSIE. Well, I wouldn't mind a cup.

LUNATIC. Don't move... I'll make it.

ELSIE. No, no. Let me. (She goes into the adjoining room, S.R.) You're not so bad once you get used to you.

LUNATIC. No, not so bad.

ELSIE. (Calls through) Were you always...?

LUNATIC. What?

ELSIE. Er... well... you know... troubled...

LUNATIC. My mind, you mean...

ELSIE. Yes... in your mind.

LUNATIC. We were very poor.

ELSIE. What a shame.

LUNATIC. No shoes. No socks. And the troikas used to go
past and shower us with filth...

ELSIE. (Pops her head round the door) The what?

LUNATIC. Troikas. One day my father, he struck the
owner... they flogged his back into strips... the dogs
were savage... so they got him.

ELSIE. Holy God!

(She pops back into the other room again)

LUNATIC. Jesus did nothing. We hung the owner by his
heels and kicked in his face. My mother died.

ELSIE. When was that dear?

LUNATIC. Before I was born.

ELSIE. Poor fella... he's not...

LUNATIC. But the workers got organised and Karl Marx
came round and gave us all presents.

ELSIE. What a nice gesture.

LUNATIC. A Jewish gentleman. He came round and handed

out presents.

ELSIE. Like Father Christmas.

LUNATIC. He said 'to hell with Jesus'.

ELSIE. What a dreadful thing to say.

LUNATIC. Yes, to small children too. He didn't care. We
loved him but we said he was bad about Jesus. He said
'Where was Jesus when the lights went out?'... and we
said... we said...

ELSIE. That's not fair. What a dreadful person.

(The LUNATIC goes to the cupboard and brings out cups
and saucers, a milk jug, sugar, spoons etc... sets
them out on the table)

LUNATIC. They got him in the end.

ELSIE. Quite right too.

LUNATIC. They got him in the end.

ELSIE. (She appears round the door) Who did?

LUNATIC. The troikas.

ELSIE. Oh, yes.

(The kettle whistles)

LUNATIC. The troikas came and got him. They did
terrible things to him and we stood and didn't say a
word. 'Papa Marx, Papa Marx,' we wanted to cry
and he wasn't brave; he screamed and screamed and
they got him in the end.

ELSIE. (Retreats again) You've had a terrible life.

(She takes off the kettle)

LUNATIC. Too bloody true.

ELSIE. That's what did it, then?

LUNATIC. What?

ELSIE. Your mind.

LUNATIC. I don't know. It's different with niggers. That's
what they say.

ELSIE. Oh, yes. They say that, do they?

LUNATIC. That's what they say.

ELSIE. (Appears with tea pot) I've made the tea.

LUNATIC. Good.

ELSIE. (Sees the table) Well, well. Cups and saucers...
and sugar as well. And milk. My, my. Who'd ever
think. You're not such a lunatic.

LUNATIC. No, not so bad... Eh?

ELSIE. I didn't say anything.

LUNATIC. I'm a humanoid telepath.

ELSIE. Are you now?

LUNATIC. You pour. I'll walk about a bit.

ELSIE. Oho.

LUNATIC. I'll walk up and down. In stir, in pokey, in the
calaboose, you get so you'd give anything just to be out
and walking... in rooms you get frantic... you can't
stand the walls...

ELSIE. There we are. Sugar?

LUNATIC. Two lumps. Yes. Niggers inside, they'll beat
their brains out and lie down, man, on the stone cold
floor and sing, slow and sad, rocking and singing, yes.

ELSIE. Oh, yes. What about that drum?

LUNATIC. Drum, drum, drum. (He is switched off)

ELSIE. What about that, then?

LUNATIC. Drum, drum, drum.

ELSIE. (Philosophically) We're on the way to making a
    right mess of our lives... and you're no help. I've seen
    some funny things in my life... (She takes some tea)
    oh yes... and I can't say I'm much bothered...
    (Another sip) but you and that Teddy take the biscuit.
    (She raises the cup to her lips and is caught by a thought.
    Long pause) You and that Teddy take the biscuit.
    (Sips her tea and thinks) You and that Teddy., you......

    (Enter DORIS, flustered)

DORIS. Teddy's been arrested.

ELSIE. What's the charge?

DORIS. I don't know.

    (Pause)

ELSIE. (With some satisfaction) I wonder what he'll get?

LUNATIC. Breach of the peace, insulting behaviour,
    soliciting, indecent exposure.

    (DORIS bursts into tears. ELSIE drinks her tea. End
    of scene)

SCENE THREE

(The same but now fully furnished in the best modern
ugly manner. Very posh. Even to having a kind of huge
white fur cover for the centre light, which makes it
look like a polar bear's testicle. Enter the SECRET
SPORTSMAN, splendid in striped trousers, black
jacket, bowler hat and umbrella, still wearing sneakers
on his feet. Followed by ELSIE, dressed as in scene I)

SPORTSMAN. Well. (Makes a large gesture) What do you
think of it?

ELSIE. Well, I never. What a change, what a transformat-
ion.

SPORTSMAN. Eh... isn't it? What d'you think of that?

ELSIE. Oh, yes. It suits you. It really does, Teddy. It's
quite...

SPORTSMAN. Just a minute. (He top-toes across the
room. Digs his feet into the white carpet) ...wall to
wall... eh.

ELSIE. Resplendent, Teddy. There's no other word for it.

SPORTSMAN. Not bad, not bad.

ELSIE. (Goes round admiring) You must have been lashing
your money around.

SPORTSMAN. Well, it was worth it. After all, what's it
for...?

ELSIE. What's this? (Goes to a large cabinet)

SPORTSMAN. Oh, that... wait a minute, though. I've got something else to show you. (He presses a switch in a small box on the table. Music plays softly) Well, what about that?

ELSIE. Gracious...

SPORTSMAN. It's all electric... I don't know what tune it's going to play till it actually plays it... it just floats out of its own accord.

ELSIE. What a set-up!

SPORTSMAN. Are you impressed?

ELSIE. Impressed... Teddy, it's overwhelming.

SPORTSMAN. It is, it is... I hoped you'd like it.

ELSIE. Oh, I do. I really do. (She is still standing by the large cabinet; she looks at it) I was saying...

SPORTSMAN. (Casually) Oh, yes, that. That is... (He presses another button in the same box) ... that.

(What is revealed is a hideous and highly colourful cocktail cabinet)

ELSIE. Oh, Teddy. The acne of luxury.

SPORTSMAN. Delighted, delighted.

ELSIE. May we...?

SPORTSMAN. Why not. A little snorter, eh, Elsie, a sort of jubilation...

ELSIE. Well, well, Teddy Chalmers. Who'd have thought it. You old fox.

(She sits down on the sofa)

SPORTSMAN. Well, old girl, what's it to be?

ELSIE. Could you manage Vodka on the rocks with a twist of lemon?

SPORTSMAN. Your wish, dear lady...

ELSIE. Ha, ha. You old fox...

SPORTSMAN. (Somewhat nonplussed by this response) Ah, well. (He pours himself a drink. Takes a cigar from a musical cigar box) Ah, well. (He perches on the side of the sofa) Ah, well. This is the life, eh, old lady?

ELSIE. You're not kidding, Teddy.

SPORTSMAN. That reminds me...

ELSIE. Oho...

SPORTSMAN. I was wondering, my dear, if I could prevail upon you to refrain from using the diminutive soubriquet, so to speak...

ELSIE. My, my. (She giggles)

SPORTSMAN. (Comes down beside her. Is very serious. Puts a hand on her knee) You know, cut out the Teddy bit and stick to calling me Edward...you know how it is.

ELSIE. Of course... Edward.

SPORTSMAN. And while we're on the subject it wouldn't do you any harm to call yourself Hermione.

ELSIE. (Tries it out) Hermione... Hermione... Well, now, Teddy... Oh, I beg your pardon... Edward (The SECRET SPORTSMAN inclines his head) ... Hermione is a very nice name...

SPORTSMAN. It's a very pretty and dignified name... er...

ELSIE. (Prompting him) Hermione.

SPORTSMAN. Hermione... (They are very pleased with themselves) So, that's settled then.

ELSIE. Well, well. So nice, so nice. (Holding up her glass) Do you think I might?

SPORTSMAN. Of course. (He gets up. Refills her glass. Swallows his own down. Pours himself another. From now on they continue to tipple steadily, getting slowly more inebriated until the scene ends) You know... Hermione... (She smiles, waggles her little finger at him) ... I don't begrudge a penny of it. Nothing but the best.

ELSIE. Teddy...

SPORTSMAN. Hermione?

ELSIE. No... but... where are they?

SPORTSMAN. They?

ELSIE. You'll get a wonderful clientele here, Edward.

(The SECRET SPORTSMAN is bemused)

ELSIE. (Gets up. Looks around) But I'd like to have a look at the girls. I hope you didn't go in for anything rather too soignee.

SPORTSMAN. (Irritably. Swallows his drink. Pours himself another. ELSIE hands over her glass. It is filled, etc.) What're you jabbering about?

ELSIE. Don't get your shirt up.

SPORTSMAN. Eh?

ELSIE. You know what I mean... what I'm telling you is from thirty years, well, twenty years' experience.

SPORTSMAN. Experience! Experience of what?... (The light begins to dawn) Do you think...

ELSIE. I know, I know, but you've got to be careful. The lower the class of person you are catering for the more soignee the girls have got to be; it's a way of getting back a bit, shoving it up a middle-class girl, it restores their dignity...

SPORTSMAN. I see what you mean, you old bag, but...

ELSIE. Whereas, Teddy, what the upper classes want is a bit of raw carrot, the stink of the potteries, a real, rough working-class bit with no holds barred. (Wisely, shaking her head) They're wrong, of course...

SPORTSMAN. How d'you mean?

ELSIE. Well, all the working-class girls I've had, they're so respectable, it's years before they're any use. Do you know, Teddy, they're so respectable they wouldn't strip for their own husbands.

SPORTSMAN. Go on!

ELSIE. It's true. No, give me a middle-class girl every time...

SPORTSMAN. I see what you mean...

ELSIE. Eh, what! They're at it like pigs in a trough. You have to watch it or they'd be working all the hours God made, God bless him.

SPORTSMAN. But, Elsie, you've got entirely the wrong end of the stick...

ELSIE. (Continuing her own thoughts) Oh, yes... Eh?... What?... you mean... oh, Teddy, I knew you were bent but has it gone this far?

SPORTSMAN. Hermione, my dear, before I fetch you one, let us drunk a toast.

ELSIE. By all means, Edward. What's it to be?

SPORTSMAN. I give you, Hermione, 'the decent life'.

ELSIE. Amen to that. And long life to the Secret Sportsman.

(The SECRET SPORTSMAN comes round. Takes
ELSIE by the shoulder and leads her to the sofa. They
sit down)

SPORTSMAN. Ah, now, that's it. That's precisely it.
(He removes his cigar, places it carefully on the table.
Takes ELSIE's hands in his, stares earnestly in her
eyes) Hermione...

ELSIE. (Somewhat vaguely) What dear?

SPORTSMAN. Hermione...

ELSIE. Well?

SPORTSMAN. Hermione...

ELSIE. Edward...

SPORTSMAN. (Swallows) When I was in prison...

ELSIE. I'm listening, Edward.

SPORTSMAN. Er... when I was in prison...

ELSIE. That was terrible, Teddy...

SPORTSMAN. I think I'll have another drink...

ELSIE. Same again, Teddy.

SPORTSMAN. That's the style...

ELSIE. Don't forget the lemon...

SPORTSMAN. No, no, there we are... that's how you like
it... (He brings her her drink. Pours himself one,
begins to pace up and down. A pause) You like the new
decor, don't you...?

ELSIE. Very tasteful, Teddy, it really is.

SPORTSMAN. Yes. I'm glad about that, er, Hermione. Because I've got a real bastard of a decision to make.

ELSIE. Oh?

SPORTSMAN. Well, that's a funny way to put it, Hermione, but you see... (He sits down again) ... you see, Hermione, it all happened when I was in prison...

ELSIE. (Rather fuddled by now) We worried about you, Teddy...

SPORTSMAN. You've got a big heart.

(ELSIE gets up. Crosses the room, goes out S. R.)

SPORTSMAN. Where are you going?... Oh...

ELSIE. Well, you've only got a few friends given in this life. They're worth husbanding.

SPORTSMAN. Eh?

ELSIE. Friends are hard to come by.

SPORTSMAN. Well, anyway, Elsie, I did a lot of hard thinking in prison. Being behind bars it stops the motion in things.

(ELSIE pulls the chain, sounds of plumbing)

You get to stand still and cluster your thought a bit.

ELSIE. What's that, dear? (She reappears)

SPORTSMAN. I was saying I did a lot of hard thinking when I was in prison, Hermione.

ELSIE. (Helping herself to another drink) It's matured you, Teddy.

SPORTSMAN. Exactly. I'm grateful to that magistrate. (ELSIE takes his glass. Refills it) When he sentenced me to three years in Holloway I nearly fainted... but after a while I began to see it was all for the best.

(He stares ahead, thinking. Very serious. ELSIE looks
down at him. A pause)

ELSIE. How did you manage with the baths?

SPORTSMAN. Oh, well, there are methods. I was a bit
hard put to it at first but once they recognised their
mistake they realised what a lot of fools they'd look
if they admitted it. So I had an easy time and no harm
done.

ELSIE. That's a blessing, anyway. You always did manage
to land on your feet Teddy.

SPORTSMAN. Anyway, I knew too much. There's dukes and
bishops in this land who'd blow their tops if ever I got
my memoires in the papers.

ELSIE. You should write it up. You've got a literary bent.

SPORTSMAN. I got to thinking, though. I got to weighing it
all up. I chummed up with one of the screws, a big,
busty girl, about forty, very strong and capable. We
used to work out together. She was a fine woman.

ELSIE. There's good and bad.

SPORTSMAN. Quite so... Anyway, we got on fine and one
day she said 'Why don't you go straight, darling?' It
struck me like a hammer.

ELSIE. Did it?

SPORTSMAN. I thought, all these years, following that
bloody lunatic and he never breathed a blind word. Not
once. You'd think, after all I've done for him, he'd've
let on. Just a simple phrase: 'Why don't you go straight,
darling?' and he never uttered it.

ELSIE. (Sits down beside the SECRET SPORTSMAN and
says very seriously) Well, I've always said, Teddy,
that lunatic is a definite trouble-maker. You remember

how it was with me.

SPORTSMAN. None so blind, Elsie... anyway, I realised
at once that that was the answer. I realised at once
that if you're to make a go of politics and that you've
got to go straight, you've got to show people you're
as straight as a die. Or at least you've got to give them
that impression. You have got to provide the
circumstances under which it is possible for them to
come to that point of view.

(After this sentence he stares at ELSIE with round-
eyed satisfaction)

ELSIE. It's not what you are, Teddy, it's what you look
like that matters. I've said that hundreds of times.
Dress it up, I've said, put a bit of colour on the meat.
If it's alright on top, if the allure's there, by the time
they've got to the bottom they're all shagged out and
happy and they don't bloody care, Teddy.

(By this time they are a fair way on. The SECRET
SPORTSMAN is seized with the beauty of it all. He
grabs ELSIE and they prance round the room together,
the SECRET SPORTSMAN singing or chanting)

SPORTSMAN. They don't bloody care, Teddy
They don't bloody care,
They don't bloody care, Teddy,
They don't bloody care.

(They collapse, laughing and giggling with oohs and
aaahs onto the sofa. Then the SPORTSMAN goes solemn
again)

SPORTSMAN. So there it is, Hermione. It's a big step. The
only question is how to go about it. Hermione. Hermione.

(ELSIE has been crooning the words 'You don't bloody
care, Teddy' and laughing to herself)

ELSIE. What's that, Teddy, dear? You don't bloody care.

SPORTSMAN. I was saying, Hermione, it's a big step.

58

ELSIE. Well, everybody has their own way of going on.
Definitely.

SPORTSMAN. I mean the thought of... you know... hitch-
ing myself up to that point of conjugality...

ELSIE. (Suddenly all attention) You mean...?

SPORTSMAN. Marriage. I've got to settle down with some
bint and make a go of it.

ELSIE. (Shrewdly) Marriage, eh!

SPORTSMAN. Yes, and Hermione I brought you round to
ask you... to put it to you...

ELSIE. (Softly, leaning towards him) Yes, Teddy...

SPORTSMAN. I mean, I know you've got my welfare at
heart, Elsie, and we've been close these many years...

ELSIE. We've been very close, Teddy.

SPORTSMAN. Of course we have. As close as two people
can be in this life...

ELSIE. Amen, Teddy.

SPORTSMAN. So what I wondered was... how d'you think
I ought to go about it?

ELSIE. Well, what you ought to know first is, is the... er
... lady willing, Teddy?

SPORTSMAN. Yes, now that's going to the heart of it. I
ought to have it all very nice and respectable and I want
her to have the best. I mean, supposing... supposing
I went down on my knees, like this... would that be the
way?

ELSIE. (Tenderly) I think so, dear...

SPORTSMAN. (Suiting action to words) I'd take her hands
in mine...

ELSIE. You would, yes, you would...

SPORTSMAN. I'd put one hand on her soft womanly
        bosom...

ELSIE. Oh, darling...

SPORTSMAN. Sort of get her all excited in a womanly
        way and I'd say... 'love of my life...'

ELSIE. Teddy...

SPORTSMAN. Hush now, I'm practising... 'Love of my
        life', I'd say, 'here kneels someone whose heart is
        flowing with the milk of human kindness...

ELSIE. Ah!

SPORTSMAN. (Frowns. Repeats the last bit) 'Milk of
        human kindness'... er... yes... 'I had a good mother
        and I never looked to see her like'.

ELSIE. That's beautiful, Teddy.

SPORTSMAN. (Grimly) 'Never looked to see her like'.
        (Takes a deep breath) 'But you and me, lovey,
        shacked up on the stream of life, will float into God's
        harbour on a kiss and a prayer. If you consent, my
        love, my life is made a beautiful and wonderful thing;
        I'll go into politics and before you know where you are
        I'll be on television   telling the bastards what's what
        and I'll probably get elected at the first shot.'

        (This last bit is said in a more natural tone as his
        thoughts suddenly drift from the proposal)

ELSIE. No doubt of it, my little hero, none whatsoever...

SPORTSMAN. That's what she'd say, d'you think?

ELSIE. She'd be a fool if she didn't.

SPORTSMAN. You know, then, you know how she feels?

60

ELSIE. I know it here, Teddy, where the deep impression of your finger still is...

SPORTSMAN. So what I'll say is straight out... 'will you be my lawful and legalised wife, yes or no?'

ELSIE. And she'll say 'yes'.

SPORTSMAN. Well, that's weight off my chest.

(He gets up from his knees, sits back)

ELSIE. (Overwhelmed) Oh dear, oh dear. I'll need a trunk full of new clothes. It's a new beginning, Teddy.

SPORTSMAN. What worries me, though, Elsie, is that bloody lunatic.

ELSIE. Oh, I shouldn't worry about him... husband... we haven't seen hair nor hide of him since you went inside.

SPORTSMAN. Just pissed off, did he?

ELSIE. Without so much as a by-your-leave.

SPORTSMAN. Did he say where he was going?

ELSIE. Not him. Just gave one of those looks of his and went off with that... drum thing of his.

SPORTSMAN. Mmmm. It wouldn't surprise me if he hadn't gone off to Tibet.

ELSIE. That's where tha yaks come from, Teddy. A very fierce tribe.

SPORTSMAN. (Bitterly) Tibet is probably where he's finished up.

ELSIE. Good riddance to bad rubbish.

SPORTSMAN. (Wistfully) He likes the Chines, you see.

ELSIE. Slant-eyed devils.

SPORTSMAN. He might have picked up quite a bit of wisdom out there. You never know.

ELSIE. Now, Teddy...

SPORTSMAN. Oh, you're right, you're right. It was guidance and knowledge I was looking for and I looked to him to give it. But no, it's all selfishness. Me in prison and him gallivanting off to Tibet. Getting himself full up with Eastern wisdom. It's bloody injustice.

ELSIE. We'd better start making plans...

(She begins to sniffle)

SPORTSMAN. I've got big plans all laid out... Here... what's up, old lady?

ELSIE. Oh, Teddy, I never thought, never... I never thought...

(She begins to boo-hoo)

SPORTSMAN. Now, now, no sniffling. It puts a damper on things, sniffling. Just you cheer yourself up. I mean, it's not so bad, is it?

ELSIE. Bad! It's marvellous, Teddy.

SPORTSMAN. What?

(She dries her tears. Smiles. Is a brave, happy, young girl)

ELSIE. Would you do me a great big favour?

SPORTSMAN. (Cautiously) Er... what sort of favour?

ELSIE. Just a teen-weeny favour for little Elsie?

SPORTSMAN. (Even more cautiously) Depends what it is.

ELSIE. Teddy, I feel really solemn at this moment...

SPORTSMAN. Solemnity costs nothing...

ELSIE. Really... you... deep down, Teddy, I feel... oh
... sacramental.

SPORTSMAN. I know what you mean.

ELSIE. Would you, could you, Teddy...?

SPORTSMAN. Spit it out.

ELSIE. Well, Teddy, I never thought it would happen and
it has. This is a bright moment, so would you just get
down with me here and now in this little love-nest and
say a prayer of thanksgiving to the Giver of All Things.

SPORTSMAN. I respect that suggestion and I'm not too
proud to say I will.

(They get down on their knees together)

ELSIE. Will you speak to Him or will I?

SPORTSMAN. Go ahead. I'm a little rusty.

ELSIE. Alright. (She composes herself) Dear Sir, I
never thought, after the way I've been going on, not to
mention my dear husband-to-be Teddy...

SPORTSMAN. (Amazed) Eh, what, your what, you mad
old bag of pus, you?

ELSIE. Teddy, you're on your knees.

SPORTSMAN. And I'll soon get off them. (He remains
kneeling) Did you hear that? Did you hear what she
said? Oh, dear, oh... (He is suddenly convulsed by
the absurdity of the idea, the pretension) ... I'm
going to bust my gut... I can't help it... my gut's
going... my gut, my gut... 'Dear Sir'... you never...
you never... Jesus... Oh, dear, oh, dear...

ELSIE. (Turns on him) You, you... I'll murder you,
Teddy Chalmers... I'm going for your eyes...

(She leaps at him)

SPORTSMAN. (Still convulsed) Oh, oh... what're you
doing? Mercy. I can't defend myself... I've ricked
myself laughing... oh, God... marry me, you greasy
old whore bag, marry me... hee, hee... aaaah,
aaaaaah...

(She has grabbed him in a bad place)

ELSIE. That's the last pleasure you'll ever know... the
last pleasure... ooooooh...

(The SECRET SPORTSMAN has retaliated)

SPORTSMAN. You bitch... you'll go for that... you'll go
... you'll go...

ELSIE. Help... help... Doris... for God's sake.

(DORIS enters in a rush)

DORIS. What're you doing?

SPORTSMAN. (Panting) Can't you see? Come back when
it's all over.

DORIS. (Tugging at him) You ought to be ashamed of yourself, you brutal animal... Just out of Holloway and this
is the way you behave.

(She tugs at his hair)

SPORTSMAN. Aaaah... let it go... let it...

(It, the hair, comes off in her hand, revealing the
polished dome beneath)

DORIS. My God... it's somebody else's... oh Lord, fancy
that!

(She begins to laugh)

SPORTSMAN. Give me that... will you give me that?

64

(She holds it out to him and he grabs at it. She retreats, dangling it in front of her)

SPORTSMAN. It's not fair. It's not fair.

(He begins to weep)

(The LUNATIC enters. He drums and drums until they are all still and staring at him... Then the SECRET SPORTSMAN grabs his wig and puts it back on. They are still)

LUNATIC. Peace be unto you. All in this holy place. For all places are holy.

ELSIE. (Grimly, from the floor) I wish he'd mind his own business.

(End of scene)

SCENE FOUR

(The same, the room in darkness, save, perhaps, for
the glow of the fire. Seated before it, the glow on his
face, the LUNATIC, the drum on his knees. During the
following words he finger-taps his drum, as a sad,
military accompaniment to the words. The rhythm as
for a slow march)

LUNATIC. I sat on the sodding ground and it was sodding
wet. The sodding rain came down and down. It was
bleak and drear. Bleak and drear it was. Jerry was
there beside me, all sodding still. The leaves did not
move, nor was there sound, but the rain came sodding
down and it was wet. Where is the glory in it and the
fine things that occur? Jerry spoke not. Jaldi, jaldi,
I said, tum bahut achachha admi ho, mourn not, neither
fail nor fear, it takes more than the sodding rain to still
a trooper's heart. But he answered me not, for his long,
sad, face, under his beaver, mourned, and his body was
still. We did not budge nor stir. The landscape was
most drear and it was bleak. Sod it, said I, sod all the
hours that brought us to this place. And Jerry said
'Aye'. So, on that bleak morning, the end of the year,
we sat on the sodding ground, and waited and waited.
And the still-warm ghosts trooped round and round
dragging their banners, tried to pass by in the best
manner, but their lips were sealed. I jumped to my
feet and armed only with a sodding umbrella I charged.
I charged over the wet turf like Spring Jack Naked
and was knifed, harpooned, blown to smithereens and
thoroughly crest-fallen. The next time I thought, the
next time, where will I be? With my oppo Jerry and all
good friends, downing the sodding good beer and
chaffing the birds. But Jerry said 'no'; with his ripped-

up face and hollowed-out belly; Jerry said 'no'... said 'no'. Doolallitap, we are, doolallitap.

(Pause. Then DORIS, in bed with the SECRET SPORTS-MAN, whispers)

DORIS. Tinker... is that you, Tinker? I know you can talk ... I heard you. Teddy wants to have me, Tinker; he had me in this bed, he wants me to marry him... isn't that terrible? Isn't that just... terrible? He's far from my ideal, you know, a long way short of it. He's lying here now, with his mouth open and his wig's come off. It's a blessing I can't see him... it really is. Tinker... are you listening?

(The LUNATIC gives a tap on his drum. This is the nearest she gets to a communication with him)

Would you give me some advice? Would you just say something? I can't speak any louder because he might wake up and that might antagonise him. I know you're jealous and everything... you're bound to be... but that's ridiculous... what Teddy does... all the time... in this bed... is neither here nor there... It's not something between us... are you listening?

(LUNATIC taps once on the drum)

Well, that's good because it's time you took hold of yourself, it really is, because there's some sense in what she says... I mean, I just couldn't marry Teddy, I just couldn't, but you must see the advantages... it'd all be laid on... if you see what I mean... dresses by the score, dining off gold plates, cut glass, Ascot every week-end, palatial surroundings... I'd never want more... and he's not without kindness...

(One tap)

... if only you'd not just sit there and not say any-thing...

(She gets up, dressed as in scene one, knickerbockers etc.)

... The trouble is... you just can't ignore everything
... You may well ask, Tinker, you may well say to
yourself 'Why does she hesitate'... It's the big chance,
the bubble, the lot... 'What does it matter' you're
telling me, aren't you, love, 'What does it matter?'
'She'll be lonely cuddled up to Teddy Bare Bum all the
days of the night... and anyway', you're saying, 'I can
manage without her and she doesn't need me, no, not a
bit of it, not a little bit of it' with your lovely face and
your lovely skin... what I want is just one good thing...
one good thing... It's only because I can't get near
you, nobody gets near you, that's the trouble, because
if we ever did get so close... Tinker... you'd be able
to feel me and that'd be nice, nice, and nice and nice...
We'd just have to touch... we'd have to...

(One smart tap on the drum)

... kisses are sacred, you know, oh, yes, I've learnt
that, kisses and cuddling... it's a secret meeting,
nobody'll know... you'll enjoy it...

(One tap)

... you will... oh, not at first, maybe,

(Tap)

the first is horrible...

(Tap, tap)

... like ripping you open...

(Tap, tap, tap)

... such savagery...

(The tapping begins here to be continuous, slowly at
first, getting faster and faster as DORIS's remarks
come faster and faster)

... he was a brute, that chap, an absolute brute, but
even then once you've got the taste for it, once you've

68

got over the hump eh, Tinker, you will, honest, just a
touch from Doris, it's like a lonely dying, oh, I
wouldn't hurt a flea, just a touch... eh... Tinker, eh,
eh...

(She has drawn her face very close to his. She puts her
arms on his, he remains rigid, turns his head, they
stare at each other for a second, slowly stand, they
move back, out of the light. DORIS says, lightly,
nervously)

DORIS. Tinker... Tinker... aaaaahh...

(Sound of a struggle; DORIS, half-choked, or squeezed
to death, shrieks)

DORIS. No, no, you're too violent, love, too... leave me
alone, leave me alone, I didn't know, Tinker, I
didn't, I...

(The SECRET SPORTSMAN wakes up, jumps out of bed.
There is the sound of beating, the SECRET SPORTS-
MAN saying:)

SPORTSMAN. Damn it, damn it again and again... all my
plans, all my schemes.

(Silence. The SECRET SPORTSMAN moves over to the
light switch, muttering)

SPORTSMAN. Ah, well, that's it, then, all finished, all
over...

(He switches on the light. DORIS is sitting on the floor,
rubbing her neck, shivering. The LUNATIC stares,
blood-stained again, holding his drum to his chest)

SPORTSMAN. Caput... done. All buggered up. What a
fiasco!

LUNATIC. Drum, drum, drum.

(The SECRET SPORTSMAN looks up with interest.
Grabs his wig from the bed. Grabs his track-suit,

puts on his sneakers. Dresses himself)

SPORTSMAN. Are you starting again? Are you in working order again? My God, you're a marvel. Was there ever a one like you? I can feel you're about to broadcast; the message is coming out loud and clear. Speak up, let it rip, let it sound forth...

(The LUNATIC taps his drum. Begins to depart, reciting the following:)

LUNATIC. The insects came in two by two,
With their staring eyes and their limbs askew.
The insects came into the ark
Where everything was cold and dark,
The insects found a place to hide
And then they committed insecticide,
And then they committed insecticide,
And then they committed insecticide.

(He exits on the repetition, his voice fading away. The SECRET SPORTSMAN is frantic and irresolute, looks at the forlorn DORIS, still shivering, holding her cap in her hands and twisting it)

SPORTSMAN. He's going to India... or Pakistan... or Japan. You just can't tell... I can't stay... much as I'd like to... much as I want to... you must under-stand... the fascination... the charm... (Calls out) ... hang on... (To DORIS by way of explanation) it's all those dhotis... (Calls out to the LUNATIC) Wait for me... I admire you, I really do... I'm impressed with all you say... (Glances back at DORIS) ... sod it... sod it... (Goes, slams the door after him)

(DORIS uses her schoolcap as a handkerchief... Blows her nose on it absent-mindedly. She puts the tip or nail of her left forefinger on her left eye tooth)

DORIS. (Recites) There was a young girl of Lent
Whose love was with lunacy bent,
But the man of her shame
Had a different name,

So instead of remaining, he went...

(A tap on the door, very tentative. ELSIE opens it, peers in)

ELSIE. Teddy, Teddy... I've recovered my equilibrium, Teddy.

DORIS. Teddy's not here.

ELSIE. (Comes into the room) I can see that.

DORIS. He's gone...

ELSIE. He'll be back.

DORIS. No, he won't, he's following that lunatic to India... or Japan... or somewhere.

ELSIE. He'll be back, I tell you... he can't keep away... (She makes a large gesture) ... his destiny is inter-twined... ah, well, I'll just rest my bones. (Looks at DORIS) Well, don't look so down in the dumps... it's nothing to look so down in the dumps about.

DORIS. (Sullenly) I'm not down in the dumps.

ELSIE. Oh, yes, you're down in the dumps alright... I can tell by the symptoms. It's pre-natal depression, that's what it is.

DORIS. What?

ELSIE. You can't hide it from old Elsie, dear. You'll be blown up like a Michelin tyre soon. I've seen it coming on, oh, yes, don't tell me there isn't a royal old bunny in your oven...

DORIS. Don't be soft...

ELSIE. I can tell... it's the shining light, it shows all round you... this baby's going to be a real challenge ... he'll inherit millions...

71

DORIS. Leave me alone...

ELSIE. Millions. There's capital set aside. There's no gentleman in the land won't be too proud to greet him.

DORIS. People don't half like to rack each other... have you got any racks... I've got a few people I'd like to rack up on them...

ELSIE. (Comforts her) There, there, dear. (Helps her to the sofa) It's a woman's destiny, it's what we all come to... some of us... men must work, women must weep. It's a wonderful system.

DORIS. India, Pakistan, or Japan. You just can't tell.

ELSIE. (Sententious) It's the thing you and Teddy have managed to do for each other... We'll have a wonderful future, did you know that? Doris, babies are the future. Every birth is an exfoliation of the infinite out of the mess of time.

DORIS. Babies are horrible.

ELSIE. (Firmly) Babies are the future.

DORIS. Drum, drum, drum. Drum... drum... drum...

VIBRATIONS

VIBRATIONS was first performed by the Edinburgh University Drama Society in September 1968 with the following cast:

A	John Pickering
B	David Edgar
C	Steve Morrison
D	Tom Hudson

The play was directed by Tony Aldgate.

(When the play opens B is examining his contraption.
A is lying on his bed, seemingly asleep. B sighs, looks
down at the floor beside his chair, picks up a screw-
driver and pokes into the contraption, then gives a
grunt of satisfaction, smiles to himself, switches it
on and begins to depress the pedal rapidly. The lights
flash, the contraption whines and shudders slightly.
After a moment or two A stirs and then suddenly sits
bolt upright. He starts forward in surprise, turns
towards B, blinks, yawns, stretches. B pedalling
furiously, speaks warmly to his contraption.)

B. Aren't you a beautiful thing? Aren't you a beautiful
thing... What a beauty... What an object... Ho, ho...
No, more than an object... you're more than a thing
... you're a contraption... Yes, a contraption...
Ha, ha, ha.

(Pedals furiously. Silence except for the whine and
the shudder and then...)

A. Stop doing that.

B. Doing what?

A. What you're doing.

B. What for?

A. I want to tell you something.

B. I can hear just as well doing it as not doing it.

A. Yes, but listen, I want your undivided attention.

(B stops)

B. Well, you've got it; what do you want to tell me?

(Pause)

A. I can't remember.

B. Oh, my God!

A. No, don't start that again. Give me a minute. I'm bound to remember if you give me a minute. But I won't remember if that thing's going on.

B. I don't see why not. We can't just sit and stare at each other until you remember.

A. Just this once you can. (Pause) Listen, I remember now. What I was to tell you was, you're not to do that.

B. What?

A. What you were doing just now. There's been a complaint.

B. A complaint? Who's complained? There's not much noise.

A. No, it's not the noise he's complaining about. It's the vibration. He says the vibration moves all the china about on his sideboard and the stuff on his mantlepiece keeps falling on the floor. Well, that's what he says.

B. But there can't be any vibration. Look! (Jumps up and down) Watch the mantelpiece. See if anything moves. (Jumps) Is anything moving?

A. No.

B. There you are then. There's no vibration.

A. Well, I said I'd tell you.

76

B. He can go and get stuffed. Why doesn't he come and see me if he's got a complaint? Why does he always go to you? I know why he always goes to you. He goes to you because he knows you're soft and you'll keep on at me until I stop.

A. There may be something in that. I've noticed when anything is wrong he always comes to me.

B. That's right. They know they can put on you, and they know you can put on me, if they can't, and that's how they get their way. But they're not getting their way this time. I'm going to do it whatever he says.

(B goes on doing it. The other reclines on the bed and begins reading his paper, then puts it down.)

A. If there's no vibration how do you account for all that stuff falling off his mantlepiece?

B. I don't account for it. I don't even consider it. If there's no vibration it's nothing to do with me.

A. Yes, but there must be some explanation.

B. Why must there be some explanation? Perhaps it just happened.

A. It couldn't just happen. Nothing just happens.

B. Of course it does. (Looks at A) You remember when you lost that collar stud? You remember? You were standing beside the bed and you lost it.

A. So I did.

B. Well, have you found it yet?

A. No I haven't found it yet. But I will though. It must be somewhere.

B. There's no 'must' about it. It's vanished, that's all. You'll never find it. We looked , didn't we? We looked for nearly an hour. Didn't we have the beds out, didn't

we strip the beds? Didn't we look all over the floor?
Didn't we?

A. Yes.

B. And we didn't find it. Did we?

A. No.

B. Well then, it's vanished. Gone. It's not anywhere. Like
the things on his mantelpiece. They just fall off. And
the same with the things on his sideboard. He's just
looking for somebody to blame, that's all, and he's not
going to blame me.

    (Pause)

A. Perhaps the vibrations don't affect our mantelpiece.
Perhaps it shows itself somewhere-else in the room.

B. Alright. You watch the rest of the room. See if it
vibrates. Ready?

A. Yes.

B. (Jumps) Well?

A. No.

B. Ready?

A. Yes.

B. (Jumps) Well?

A. No.

B. Ready?

A. Yes.

B. (Jumps) Well?

A. No, not there.

B. Ready again?

A. Yes.

B. (Jumps) Any vibrations?

A. No.

B. Well, that's the whole room and there's no vibration.

A. It certainly looks like it.

B. There you are then. Can I get on with it now?

A. I suppose so.

(He goes back to the bed and begins reading his paper.
B. begins again. There is a sound of footsteps coming
upstairs. A. puts down his paper slowly and listens)

A. It's him.

B. Who's him?

A. From downstairs. He's coming up.

B. Damn! What's he want?

A. It must be about the vibrations.

B. Well, if it's a row he's after he's come to the right
place. There aren't any vibrations, so if he's looking
for trouble he'll get it.

(Knock)

B. What d'you want?

C. Open the door.

B. What d'you want?

C. I'll tell you that when you open the door. I've got a pail
full of smashed china here, and a clock, and a vase.

79

B. So? What do you expect me to do about it?

C. Open the door. (Hammering) Open the door.

B. Open the door.

(A. gets off the bed, goes over and opens the door.
C. pushes his way in)

C. Look at this! China, clocks, vases. All your fault.

B. Hang on. Don't adopt that tone of voice with me. It
may be alright for some people but when you're talking to me try and keep your voice down.

C. I am keeping my voice down. It's your doing that. It
causes vibrations.

B. No, it doesn't.

C. How do you account for all this then?

(He empties the pail on the floor)

C. There's a lot of money here. I sit down for a smoke
and a read and then you start and all these things start
dancing up and down and before I can stop them they're
on the floor.

B. Nothing to do with me. This room's as solid as...;
well look, try it yourself. Jump up and down.

C. What?

B. Jump up and down.

C. What do you take me for?

B. Jump up and down. If there's vibrations from doing
this, there'll be vibrations from doing that. That's
reasonable, I suppose.

C. (Reluctantly) I suppose so.

(Jumps)

B. There. You see.

C. No, I didn't see. You jump and I'll look.

B. We'll all bloody well jump. If we jump round and round, the three of us, we'll see if there's any vibrations. If three of us can't make any vibrations, there aren't any.

(They jump, harder and harder, turning round all the time. Nothing stirs)

B. Well?

C. That doesn't prove anything. There are kinds of vibrations. Jumping didn't crack that glass, did it?

B. No. Nobody said it would.

C. Ah, but if you were to sing or whistle a certain note it would.

A. I have heard that.

B. It's well known. So?

C. Well then. It's doing that that causes the vibrations, not jumping.

B. Alright, alright. I'll tell you what. He'll do it and you go downstairs with me and see if there's any vibrations.

C. Alright then. I can't keep going on at this rate.

B. You know what to do?

A. I should do. I've watched you doing it often enough.

B. Wait till we get downstairs. I'll shout and then you start doing it. Right?

A. Right.

b. Come on, then.

   (They go downstairs)

B. (Shouts) Ready?

A. Yes.

B. Go, then.

   (A. begins to do it)

B. Are you doing it?

A. Yes, I'm doing it.

B. Do it harder. Do it as hard as you can.

A. I am.

B. (Triumphantly) Alright, stop.

   (Footsteps are heard coming up the stairs)

B. I told you it wasn't that.

C. Does he do it the same way as you do it?

B. Of course he does. It can't be done in any other way.

C. That's what you say. You'd be bound to say that. You do it and we'll watch.

   (They arrive back in the room)

B. Alright, it's all the same to me. Give me the signal.

   (A. and C. go downstairs. B. waits. There is a cry of triumph)

C. There.

(A crashing sound follows this and then another. A. and C. come rushing upstairs)

C. I told you, I told you. As soon as you started, it started.

B. I didn't start. I haven't even moved.

C. I knew you'd say that. Well, let me warn you. . .

B. Let me warn you. . .

C. I'm telling you. Cut it out. If there's any more of it there'll be trouble.

B. Look here, you're just asking for trouble, aren't you?

C. I've told you. That's flat. Once more and you look out.

(C. goes out, slamming the door. B. collects the pieces of china in the pail, opens the door and throws it out)

B. And take your broken bits with you.

(Slams the door. End of scene.
Lights go down and come up, but dimly. They are in bed)

A. Listen. Wake up. Listen.

B. What? What? What's the matter?

A. Can't you hear it, feel it, I mean?

B. Feel what? Hear what?

A. Vibrations.

B. Don't you start.

A. But I can feel it. Can't you feel it?

B. Feel it where?

A. The bed. The bed's vibrating.

B. I can't feel any vibrations.

A. It is, I tell you. Lie still. Relax.

(Pause)

There. It's vibrating.

B. Well, I did think I felt something. Get out and feel it with your hand. Feel the rail. Go on.

A. Alright.

(Gets out of bed)

B. Well, can you feel anything?

A. I don't know. Maybe it's me, you see. My hand's not steady.

(A crash. Two objects fall from the mantelpiece)

B. Good God! You're right.

A. I told you, I told you.

B. It's him. It's that bastard downstairs. He's got something running down there. I'll kill him. He's started to do it because he thinks I'm causing vibrations. Either that or he wants this room. He's always had his eye on this room. His is not a patch on ours.

(Another crash)

B. I'll get him. I'll soon stop his little caper.

(A door is heard to open, shut, and feet are heard going downstairs)

B. There, he's gone.

(Another crash)

B. He's left it running. Come on. Let's go down and stop it. He won't get away with this. Fancy him thinking I'd let him get away with a thing like that.

A. We won't be able to get in.

B. We can listen, anyway. We'll hear it running.

A. Come on then.

B. After me.

(They go downstairs. Their whispering voices can be heard)

B. Put your ear to the keyhole.

A. It's got dust in it.

B. (Impatiently) Blow through it then.

(A. blows)

B. Put your eye to it; see if you can see it.

(Pause)

B. Well, can you see it?

A. It's a mess alright.

B. (Impatiently) Can you see it?

A. It's dark. I have to wait for the sign outside to light it up.

B. Well?

(Pause)

A. No... no. Nothing.

B. You can't see the whole room.

A. No, I can't see the whole room. How do you expect me to see the whole room through the keyhole with no light on?

B. It's there, though. It could be under the bed or on either side of the door.

A. Well, I can't see it.

B. Here, let me. I'll listen for it. Shh.

A. I'm not making a noise.

B. I can hear you breathing.

A. I can hear you breathing.

B. It doesn't matter what you can hear. You're not listening. Stop breathing. Good. Good.

A. Can you hear anything?

B. I think so. Yes, I think so.

A. What's it like?

B. Funny. Like a kind of sea-shell sound, or singing sound.

A. Let me.

B. Here you are, then.

A. Stop breathing. Yes. I can hear something.

B. That's it, then. Come on.

A. Where?

B. We're going in.

A. What, into his room?

B. Into his room. We have a right. He's committed a

86

breach of the peace. He's a public nuisance. He's breaking the law. All citizens have a right to enforce the law.

A. Have they?

B. Of course they have. Suppose... Never mind. Come on.

(The sound of a door being smashed open. A. shouts)

B. You look under the bed.

(The noise of furniture being moved about)

B. Found anything?

A. No.

B. Me neither.

A. He's got it well hidden. Whatever it is.

B. No. It's no good. We've got to be rational. It's not here.

A. Where is it, then?

B. I don't know. It's not here. Nowhere. There isn't anything.

(They shut the door and are heard coming upstairs)

B. There isn't anything.

A. What about the sound?

B. Sound?

A. The sound we heard when we listened.

(They come into the room)

B. Stop breathing.

A. Again!

B. Yes, stop breathing.

A. What for this time?

B. So I can listen.

A. You don't think he's planted it here?

B. No. Planted it here? No. I want to listen.

A. What for?

B. You'll see.

A. Alright.

   (Pause)

B. Ah!

A. What?

B. I heard it again.

A. That sound?

B. Yes.

A. Let me try.

B. Alright.

A. Stop breathing.

B. Right.

   (Pause)

A. Yes. Yes. I can hear it. Where does it come from?

B. It doesn't come _from_ anywhere. It's here all the time.

88

A. Here, why here?

B. Not here especially. Everywhere.

A. Everywhere? You mean there's always a noise, even
    when it's quiet, and we've never heard it before?

B. We never listened before.

A. Well, what is it?

B. It's us. I think.

A. Us?

B. Yes. We carry the sound about with us. It's the blood.
    Our blood. It's the blood in our ears. It's the activity
    of our brain. All the time. Hmmmmm. Quiet sinister
    bloody machinery humming away all the time.

A. It can't be.

B. It is. Listen.

    (Both hold their breath)

BOTH. Horrible!

    (Both stand, listening. A sudden crash of crockery
    from the sideboard)

A. It's started again. It's him. It must be him.

B. It's not him.

A. Has it stopped?

B. Feel the bed rail again.

A. I can't. I'm shaking.

B. YOU'RE NOT SHAKING.

A. I am shaking. Look.

                                                        89

(Holds out his hand)

A. It trembles.

B. You're not shaking. You're <u>vibrating</u>.

A. What?

B. Vibrating.

A. Why me? Why me vibrating?

B. Watch.

(Holds out his hand. It trembles)

B. <u>I'm vibrating as well</u>. <u>We're both vibrating</u>.

(Door opens downstairs. Then shuts. Then another. Shout. Feet come pounding upstairs. Man comes in)

C. You've broke into my room.

B. Quiet.

C. Quiet?

B. Quiet.

C. What for? What about my room?

B. We're vibrating.

C. You're off your bloody heads.

B. Hold out your hand.

C. I won't.

B. Hold it out.

C. I won't.

B. Alright. He'll hold out his hand. Watch.

90

C. Well?

B. Notice anything?

C. No.

B. Watch again.

C. It's shaking.

B. It's vibrating. Hold out your hand.

C. Alright. There.

B. See.

C. It is shaking.

B. That's right. Stand still. Feel your legs under you. Feel your head. Feel your backside. Trembling. We're all quietly trembling; being trembled.

C. Being trembled?

B. I'm not sure. Trembling. Or being trembled.

A. If we're being trembled, who's trembling us?

C. It's him. It's him and what he's doing.

B. No it isn't. I'm not doing it.

C. I'm not well.

B. You don't look well.

C. I haven't been well since the cups started to dance. I was alright till then. Never a day's illness. Woke up. Morning. Cold, warm, never bothered. Jumped out of bed. Washed, singing all the time. Then, them dancing cups and now look at me. Trembling.

B. Or being trembled.

(C. gives a cry. Door slams. Silence. They return to their respective tasks; B. to doing it, A. to his paper)

A. There's a secret centre in the universe sending out pulses of power. Yes.

(B. continues with his work)

A. A secret centre.

B. Absolute balderdash. Preposterous. Absurd. Ridiculous. Lunatic.

A. Answer me this. Is it true that only we are trembling or does everybody tremble?

B. Well, in the way we tremble, everybody does, I suppose.

A. Everybody?

B. Everybody.

A. And is this accidental?

B. It must be.

A. There's no 'must' about it. You said so yourself. Is it a likely story that everybody trembles and there's no reason for it?

B. Not a likely story.

A. Secret pulses of power. A general influence.

B. Rubbish.

A. Mmmmmm. Machinery. Feel your pulse. Listen. Stop breathing.

(Silence)

A. What can you hear?

B. Heart beating, pulse faint but fluttering. Sound in ears. General trembling.

A. All adding up to?

B. Adding up to?...

A. Messages. Messages tapped out on the brain. On the body. . . . - - -, . . . , . . . - - - . . . , . . . - - - . . .

B. For God's sake!

(Pause)

A. What happens when you programme a computer?

B. Well, you put in messages and get out information.

A. What happens when you put in self-contradictory information?

B. Well, the computer, the computer...

A. Well?

B. Vibrates.

A. It does. It vibrates. It lights up. It shakes.

B. Ah, but we're not computers.

A. Machinery. The brain's all machinery. When the machine goes wrong it trembles. It gets ataxia. You know that. It begins to vibrate. Give it a cup of tea and it shakes and shakes and shakes.

B. We are not machines. Nobody has programmed me. Nobody is sending me messages. I am not misinform-ed. There are no pulses of power.

A. It fits the facts.

(Slight pause)

B. Switch it on.

A. What do you want to switch that thing on for?

B. Switch it on. It'll take your mind off things. It'll take <u>my</u> mind off things.

A. <u>It's</u> a thing.

B. You take your mind off things by putting your mind on things.

A. Ataxia. Aim to miss and you'll hit it.

B. Switch it on.

(He switches it on. The far wall is slowly lit up with a dancing image)

A. It's vibrating!

B. Vertical hold.

(He fiddles. It still dances)

B. Horizontal hold.

(The image comes still. Reveals the giant image of a tall, distinguished, grey-haired man. He smiles. He is standing behind a table. On it are models of gryphons, centaurs, knights in armour, goblins, ladies. Beside them lies a long sword. He begins to speak, and the speech must grow from calm authority towards hysteria, in both parts, the same development)

I have been asked to speak to you on what the quiet hour means to me. This is the quiet hour. Just before darkness. I imagine you in your homely rooms looking at me whom you can see but whom I cannot observe. I am to speak to you in this quiet hour and to say what it means, what it means to me. I hope my words will find their echoes in you. I hope you will understand me and that you will yield your minds to

what I say. When I was a child I thought as a child, I
spoke as a child. But when I became a man, I put away
childish things. So Paul the Apostle. Here the language
is mild. I put them away. But the thought is fierce;
not mild. When I was a child I touched things. I fondled
them. I played in the world. I danced before it. My
mind also was stored with symbols, delicate, charming,
beautiful. I glance down at the symbols of my childhood. I did not understand. I did not understand. But
when I became a man, I destroyed my childhood. I
destroyed my memory. I broke to pieces the
absurdities of the child. I smashed my symbols.

(As he says this his voice grows shrill and he smashes
the symbols with the sword. He controls himself.
Smiles. Begins again)

Let me explain. You know, before we are born we lie
protected, warm, satisfied, in the womb. We live in
an environment exactly suited to our needs. We get
the impression that the world circles around us and
ministers to us. The world of our pre-natal experience
is the image of our desires. We are born. We carry
this impression with us. We explore. We handle things.
We caress them. Like savages we dance our joy in the
presence of the world. But this is a terrible, a fear-
ful mistake. It is not like that. It is obdurate, hostile,
inimical, it is our enemy. It is an enemy with a
thousand pleasing faces. We must smash our way
through it. We must mould it, destroy it, break it,
brand it, make it obey. We must hurl ourselves
against it in deadly hate. It is not our friend. It is the
other, standing against us, against our will, against
our need. Its ruin is our salvation. But we are
fragile. Our will is infinite but our bodies are soft;
our desires betraying. We weaken before it. We must
not weaken. We are finite but it is vast and eternal.
We destroy it, but we bleed and destroy ourselves. In
life there is no salvation. We are lost in the material,
the hard black surfaces we need to break. To live is
to destroy; to destroy is to destroy ourselves. This
we must do. Death is the triumphant affirmation of
our will to live. As we die so do we live. Join with me,
join with me then, on my pilgrimage of hate, my will

95

to life in my will to death. Join with me, friends, enemies, join with me.

(As he says this he raises his arms wide towards them. His hands are shaking. He is trembling and sweating)

B. Switch it off.

A. It wasn't good tonight.

B. Wasn't it? I wasn't listening.

A. He was shaking.

B. The man on the tele?

A. Yes, shaking like a leaf. Mind you, he was clever. There's a lot in what he says.

B. What do they know?

A. If they didn't know, why would they be asked to speak on the tele?

B. Oh, he knows somebody who knows somebody.

A. It's not like that.

B. It's a bloody rotten conspiracy.

(Pause)

A. If you look in a still pond, it's swarming, isn't it?

B. Eh?

A. Swarming.

B. So it is.

A. And look at that door.

B. What's wrong with it?

A. It's peeling. And it's darker than when we painted it.

B. So?

A. And look across the room.

B. Which way?

A. Any way. Small specks of dust. Not noticed. Slowly sifting down, cushioning and exploding on the carpet. The door was darkening all the time. The leaves aren't still, but minutely vibrating. The sand is moving. The wind is undetected. Everything is vibrating.

(Pause)

B. I like this room.

A. Yes, it's a nice room.

B. I've always liked this room.

A. Not always. You thought it was too small when we first came.

B. Well, I hadn't seen it with the furniture in it. It was alright when the furniture was in it.

A. You've never liked that mantelpiece.

B. You've never liked that chair. Come to think of it, you've never liked the way I arranged the furniture in this room, have you?

A. Well, you never listen to what I say.

B. Not if you want to arrange it the way you wanted to arrange it.

A. It would have been better my way.

B. There you are. Just what I said. You've never liked this room.

A. I liked the _room_.

B. So it's me you're objecting to.

A. You never listen to what I say.

B. You never say anything worth hearing. And another
thing, all that talk about vibrations. Stones are still,
sometimes. It's us that's vibrating. And how do you
explain all that stuff falling down?

A. It's him.

B. It's you. You don't fit in. It's obvious. Two people
vibrating. Some people don't have stuff falling off the
mantelpiece. How do you explain that?

A. They're lucky.

B. There's no luck about it. Because they fit each other
they vibrate harmoniously; _harmoniously_. You've
never really liked me and I've never really liked you.
We don't vibrate, you see. It's no good.

A. Perhaps it's him.

B. It's not him. It's you. Look what happened when I went
downstairs.

A. What, then?

B. _Nothing_. Not a bloody thing. Look what happened when
you went downstairs.

A. What?

B. Chaos! Stuff falling down all over the place. You don't
fit in.

A. Yes I do.

B. No you don't.

A. I do.

98

(Pause)

B. Poor bloody wretch.

(Pause. They come together and clasp each other.
But they both begin to tremble violently. They break
apart. There is a crash of crockery. The bed
collapses, everything starts falling, books, clothes.
The light goes out. End of scene. When the next
scene opens some attempt has been made to tidy up
the room. Both are sitting, one on either side of the
table. They are staring out towards the audience.
There is silence for a moment. B. scratches his head,
looks at his fingernails and falls to scratching his
head again. A. steals glances at B. and looks uneasy.
He twists about in his chair)

B. I must think.

A. Think, then. We must do something.

B. I am thinking.

A. Well?

B. You're not to blame.

A. How do you make that out?

B. You're completely exhonerated. You may leave the
court without a stain on your character.

A. How do you make that out?

B. It's simple; the sculpture of chance. That's what you
are, the sculpture of chance. Like a thousand delicate
little thumbs dimpling and stroking the mild surfaces
of your skin. Stands to reason.

A. You mean it's not my fault?

B. Well, it's you alright, but you're not to blame. Are
you, or are you not composed, almost entirely, with a
few acids and a lot of water, of cells?

99

A. I am.

B. You are. And are these cells like little blind animals with little blind needs?

A. They are.

B. If a great number of these little blind animals fall sick, do you fall sick?

A. I do.

B. Exactly. If they're satisfied so are you.

A. That's right.

B. So, your needs are the logical product of the sum of theirs, and your consciousness is the epiphenomenal expression of the sotto-voce desires of a conglomeration of little blind bloody blasted little animals.

A. That's what I am.

B. So you're not to blame. It's them. And they're not to blame because they don't know what the hell they are doing. So nobody is to blame and I beg your pardon for going on about you like that.

A. No offence meant and none taken.

B. It's good of you to take it like that.

A. Not at all, not at all.

(Pause)

B. It's no good.

A. What's the matter now?

B. It's not official.

A. Does it have to be official?

B. Well, it's no good just knowing that you're not to blame; it's got to be official.

A. But if you know I'm not to blame and I know I'm not to blame, it doesn't need to be official.

B. If it's not official you don't know you're not to blame. A person doesn't know he's guilty until the verdict is pronounced, does he?

A. Well, he knows whether he's done it or not.

B. That's not the same thing. The judge doesn't say 'You did it', he says, 'Guilty'. That=s what he says. And when he says 'Guilty', then the prisoner is guilty and not before.

A. Yes, I suppose so.

B. You suppose so! Of course he isn't. It has to be pronounced. Suppose he did it and he was hanged but he hadn't been pronounced. Would that be justice?

A. No, that's terrible.

B. Of course it is. It's terrible. It's a glaring injustice. He can't be hanged properly until he is pronounced guilty. Then he is guilty and he is hanged. Officially.

A. Well...

B. Well. If he's only guilty when he is pronounced, he's only innocent when he's pronounced. Q. E. D.

A. But how are we going to make it official?

B. Nothing so simple. We have to become officials.

A. And how do we do that?

B. By a duly constituted democratic procedure.

A. And how do we do that?

B. By being elected, of course.

A. Who's to elect us?

B. We are. We constitute an electorate and we elect who we like. That's democracy.

A. Who do we elect?

B. Who else but us?

A. Exactly so.

B. Do you agree to constituting a court?

A. I do.

B. Then it's done.

A. Who's the judge?

B. Well, you can't be the judge.

A. Why not?

B. Because you're the accused. It wouldn't be fair to you. You might not get the right verdict. You wouldn't be impartial. You might pronounce yourself innocent and you might be guilty.

A. But I am innocent.

B. There you are. You've made up your mind already and you haven't even heard the evidence. No, you can't be your own judge and expect to get justice. It's not in human nature.

A. I see.

B. So I'll be judge.

A. But how do I know that I'll get justice if you're the judge? At least if I'm judge I'll give myself a good hearing.

B. It's not a good hearing you want, it's a fair hearing. And you won't get a fair hearing unless I'm the judge. And that's because I'm impartial. I'll be nothing but an official. My private feelings are as nothing. Because I'm not judging myself, you see? I stand towards you as a judge towards the accused. And you can't expect to stand towards yourself in the way, now can you?

A. Well, if you say so.

B. Agreed then. I'm hereby elected judge. Who's the defence?

A. I am.

B. No you're not. That would be fatal. You'd get too excited. You might incriminate yourself. Besides, you would be pleading for yourself and everybody would think you were just putting a good face on it.

A. But I would be bound to make out a good case.

B. No you wouldn't. You might break down. And you might ask yourself the wrong questions.

A. How could I do that? I would only ask myself questions I knew the answer to.

B. Fatal. Absolutely fatal. The most important thing is not what you know but what you don't know. What you don't know proves what you didn't do. What you do know proves what you might have done.

A. Well then, I'll ask myself questions I don't know.

B. Ah. But if you don't know, how do you know what questions to ask to prove that you don't know what if you did know would prove you might have done it?

A. I don't know.

B. There you are then.

A. You be defence.

B. Right then. I am hereby duly elected defence.

A. I suppose you have to be prosecutor as well.

B. Prosecutor, me? Not at all. You be prosecutor.

A. Why me? I'm not going to ask myself incriminating questions.

B. It's not the questions that are incriminating, it's the answers. Everybody accuses themselves best. Even when they're not really guilty, they wonder whether they are or not and they blame themselves. They ask themselves questions. You're lucky. You only have to answer your own questions. I have to pronounce the verdict. That's the worst thing.

A. Alright then, I'm duly elected prosecutor.

B. Call the first witness.

A. Call the first witness.

B. You're the first witness.

A. Am I,

B. There's nobody else.

A. I haven't been accused yet. You have to read the indictment.

B. Well remembered. Go into the dock.

A. Where's the dock?

B. Where you are now. That'll do for the dock.

A. Right.

B. Prisoner at the Bar...

A. Yes.

B. You're not supposed to say anything yet.

A. Oh.

B. Prisoner at the Bar. Inasmuch as you are accused of being what you are, you are no different from anyone else. Inasmuch as you are guilty...

A. Already? But you haven't heard the evidence yet.

B. Inasmuch as you are guilty or NOT GUILTY it is in virtue of what you are, not in yourself, but qua man.

A. Qua man?

B. Qua man. You remember about the cells and that.

A. Oh yes. Qua man.

B. Qua man you are accused of vibrating to the detriment of public property and the fundamental disharmony of the human race.

A. Well put.

B. How say you? Do you plead guilty or not guilty?

A. Guilty.

B. Guilty! What do you mean 'Guilty'? You have to plead 'Not guilty'.

A. Yes, but the way you put it...

B. You're not supposed to listen to what I say. You're supposed to plead 'Not guilty' and I'll decide when I have heard the evidence. I direct the prisoner to plead 'Not guilty'.

A. Not guilty, then.

B. Now you have to give evidence. You have to be sworn in.

A. We need a book.

B. We've only got one book.

A. Where?

B. That one.

A. This is no good. It's the <u>Tractatus Logico Philosophicus</u>.

B. By Ludovic Wittgenstein. In the original translation. Read out the first proposition.

A. 'The world is everything that is the case. '

B. 'The world is the totality of facts, not of things. '

A. 'The facts in logical space are the world. '

B. 'Any one can either be the case or not be the case, and everything else remain the same. '

A. 'The feeling of the world as a limited whole is the mystical feeling. '

B. 'The world is independent of my will. '

A. 'The riddle does not exist. '

B. 'The world of the happy is quite another than that of the unhappy. Death is not an event of life. Death is not lived through. '

A. 'Whereof one cannot speak, thereof one must be silent. '

B. Well said. Do you swear to tell the truth, the whole truth and nothing but the truth, so help you Wittgenstein?

A. No.

B. Why not?

A. Well, how can I be sure that what I say is the truth?

B. Read the book.

A. In the beginning was the word.

B. Not that book. Read from the book you have got in your hand.

A. I can't read from this book. I don't understand what it says.

B. Who says what?

A. I do. I just said it. I said 'I don't understand it'.

B. Who says so?

A. I say so.

B. Who are you to say so?

A. Who am I to say so? Well...

B. Precisely. You don't know who you are to say so. Why should it be up to you to decide you don't understand?

A. Who else, who else, for God's sake!

B. Not you, anyway. Do you say <u>you</u> say when you understand? Do you?

A. Of course I do.

B. You don't. If you did how could I say to you, you don't understand when you don't understand and you think you do?

A. Do you say that?

B. I do. You don't understand.

A. Well. That's what I said. I agree with you.

B. Yes, but I'm entitled to say so. You're not. I'm the public and what the public says concerning what you understand must be true.

A. I don't see that.

B. That's because you think it's up to you to decide what you understand and what you don't. How do you know when you don't understand?

A. I don't know <u>how</u> I know. I just do. I feel queer, vague, all confused.

B. That doesn't <u>mean</u> you don't understand. I often feel like that and <u>I</u> understand.

A. How do you know?

B. It's common knowledge.

A. Is it?

B. It's well known.

(While they have been speaking the door has opened and C. and D. have entered. D. is a young, bald-headed man, dressed in a plain blue suit and dark tie. He wears thick spectacles. It is difficult to place him, to say what he is. As A. and B. talk C. walks over to what B. has been doing and fiddles. D. stares at A. and B. He tries the bed, isn't satisfied, walks up to them, stares at each in turn, listens to both attentively, then sits down and stares ahead. B. turns and notices C.)

B. Who told you to come in?

C. Nobody. The door was open. You were busy so I came in and waited. I didn't think you would want to be interrupted. I wanted to introduce you to my friend.

B. Bring him in then.

A. (Starts violently in noticing D.) There he is. Who is he?

C. My friend. May I introduce you to may friend.

B. You may. (D. takes no notice) Does he have to sit like that?

   (D. rises. Turns slowly, smiles at them. They start back)

D. How do you do?

B. Very well. That is...

A. Thank you. Very well. How do you do?

   (D. smiles. Sits down again)

B. He's no talker, is he?

C. He doesn't say much, that's true. He's none the worse for that. Still waters...

B. He's not going to do any deep running here. What does he do? What's his profession? What does he do for a living? Friend or no friend, I'm not having bald-headed young men in blue suits and goggles coming into my room, friend or no friend, and not saying anything but 'How do you do' and then sitting down and just smiling. There are rules, there are conventions. What is his place? What is he for? How are we to treat him? These questions must be answered.

C. He's something in the city.

B. A broker, you mean.

C. Not a broker, exactly.

B. A bull or a bear?

C. A bit of both, I should say.

B. A bit of both? That's a queer thing to be.

A. It is a queer thing to be.

B. I've never heard of that before.

C. A bull or a bear.

D. A bull or a bear.

B. Oh! Very surprising. Is that all he is?

C. Well, there we have it. You put me in a bit of a quandary there. You might say he has (He giggles) animal connections.

B. I don't like the sound of that.

A. We all have animal connections. There's nothing un-usual about that.

D. True, true.

B. True! True! But we don't make a profession of it. We try to ignore it as best we can. That's what we try to do. Is there anything else?

C. It's hard to say.

B. Is it? Well, whatever he is, is he good at it?

D. I do very well, thank you.

B. Glad to hear it, I'm sure. Would you say 'successful' perhaps?

D. Successful.

B. A man after my own heart. I hate people who are failures.

C. Friends, then?

B. Friends.

(He goes and shakes D. by the hand. A. does not move)

110

B. Why don't you shake the gentleman by the hand?

A. Do I have to?

B. Not so loud, not so loud. Is that any way to treat a
guest? Of course you must. Common politeness.
Common politeness.

A. Oh well. If you think so.

(He goes up to D. They stare at one another, briefly
touch hands, A. turns away)

A. It's the vibrations.

B. Are you feeling them again?

A. Don't you feel them again?

B. I've never felt so relaxed. (To D.) Sir, may I ask?
Do you feel relaxed?

D. Quite relaxed, thank you.

B. (To C.) Do you feel relaxed?

C. Now that you mention it, I do.

B. There. It's only you that doesn't feel relaxed, it
seems. Only you.

A. Why me?

B. That's what we have to decide.

A. What, now?

B. Have you forgotten the trial?

A. I did forget.

B. I didn't forget. I've had it in mind all this time. It's
fortunate, you gentlemen turning up like you did. (To
C.) Does he know about the trouble we had with the

vibrations and the cups and all that?

C. He has been informed.

B. Informed, has he? That's good then. Well, as I was
saying, it occurred to us that the cause of these
vibrations and the cups and things was my friend here.

C. Ah!

(They all look at A.)

B. My friend.

(They all look at A.)

B. Well, as I was telling you, we thought that the cause of
the trouble was my friend. Not vibrating harmoniously,
you see.

C. Ah.

B. Yes! You remember how it was when you and he went
downstairs together?

C. I do indeed. I do indeed.

B. And you remember how it was when you and I went
downstairs?

C. I do remember. No trouble at all. Everything quite
quiet, as I remember it.

B. You do remember it. So, my friend and I came to the
conclusion he was the cause of it.

C. Is that so?

B. But then, you see, it occurred to me, that if he was
the cause, he might not be to blame.

D. Not to blame.

B. That's what occurred to us. But you can't leave it like

that. We both felt that. Accusations and charges can't be dismissed so lightly.

C. I should think not indeed.

B. Exactly, exactly. We felt the need to make it official.

D. Official. Yes. Very good.

B. Splendid. So we constituted ourselves a court and the trial, in a manner of speaking, was under way, when you two gentlemen put in an appearance.

C. If we can be of any assistance...

B. Well, that is a kind thought. (To A.) Did you hear that? Indeed you can. Indeed and indeed you can. I was thinking, just before you came in. There's not enough of us. I didn't actually say anything, but I was thinking that all the same.

A. I don't like it now.

(Pause)

A. It's not the same.

B. It's not the same, it's better.

A. It's worse.

B. I was saying, it's better now. I asked myself, before you two gentlemen put in an appearance, I asked myself this question: 'What does this court require?'

D. Revenge.

B. Revenge?

D. Revenge. For all her slaughtered children. For the dead who do not ask for justice. For the living who don't understand.

A. I don't understand. I said before that I didn't under-

113

stand. Whose slaughtered children? Whose dead? I don't understand.

B. It's a joke. He's making a joke. Can't you see that? He's got a very quiet sense of humour, your friend. (To D.) It was a joke, wasn't it? (D. smiles at B.) Er... there. You see?

(B. and C. laugh. Pause)

C. Well. So there's to be a trial. If we can be of any assistance.

B. Of course you can. We were a bit short-handed, as you might say. It had the air of a contrivance. A bit <u>ad hoc.</u> I was to be judge.

D. Ah.

B. I was to be judge and I was to be defence and he was to be prosecutor.

A. Yes, it was better that way.

B. It was worse that way. Now, as I see it, you (To C.) can be defence and your friend there, if he is willing, your friend can be the prosecutor.

C. Delighted.

D. No.

B. No? Did you say 'No'?

D. Not prosecutor.

B. Ah well. It does you credit. Being prosecutor is a thankless task. If you win the case nobody thanks you and if you lose it everybody says you're a fool. Well, well. You be witness, then. We need a witness. That's what you can be.

D. Witness.

B. So let us begin.

(Unlike the first time, the preparations for the trial
are now elaborate. B. pulls out a scarlet blanket and
wraps it about him. They arrange a chair upon the
table so that he sits at the back of the stage elevated
above the others. They reverse a table in the corner
for a dock, etc. It should be so arranged that every-
one except A. in the dock is slightly in shadow)

C. Well, that's all very nice, I must say.

B. Much better, much better. Should I ascend?

C. Please do, m'lud.

B. Thank you.

(C. assists him on to the table. He seats himself)

B. (To A.) Go into the dock.

(A. goes slowly into the dock)

B. We'll take the first bit as read. Call the first witness.

D. (Comes forward) I am the first witness.

B. Take the stand. Raise your right hand. (D. raises
his right hand, fist clenched)

B. Do you swear to tell the truth, the whole truth and
nothing but the truth?

D. I swear.

B. Thank you, thank you very much. Prosecutor, you may
proceed.

(A. does nothing. He stands staring at nothing)

B. I said, 'Prosecutor, you may proceed.'

A. What?

B. Are you or are you not the Prosecutor?

A. I am.

B. Then proceed.

A. What do I do?

B. You're supposed to ask this witness questions and you're supposed to reduce the witness to a babbling lunatic by asking him questions to which there is no straight answer and requiring him to say 'yes' or 'no'. Whereupon you rest your case. It's common practice.

A. What questions do I ask?

B. You see, gentlemen; this is what we're faced with. How can a trial proceed when we're faced with the likes of that? Ask him any question you like.

A. Any questions?

B. Any question whatsoever.

A. Well then. (Turns to D.) What did you have for breakfast today?

C. Objection.

B. Upon what grounds?

C. The prosecutor is merely trying to confuse the witness by asking irrelevant questions.

B. Quite right. Objection... er... sustained.

A. What do I do now?

B. Ask him another question.

A. What did you have for lunch?

C. Objection.

B. What now?

C. The witness's gastronomical experiences are beside the point.

B. Right again. Objection sustained. Ask him another question.

A. What sort of question shall I ask him?

B. Ask him what he had for dinner.

C. Objection.

B. You are making too many objections. How is this trial to proceed if every time somebody opens their mouth to ask an interesting question you bob up and object?

C. As your lordship pleases.

B. His lordship does please. Ask him what he had for dinner.

A. What did you have for dinner?

D. Food.

B. That's no sort of answer to a civil question. Ask him again.

A. What did you have for dinner?

D. Food.

A. And tea?

C. Objection.

B. Silence.

D. Food.

A. And lunch?

B. What did you have for lunch?

D. Food.

B. Did you have fried onions and chips and liver?; something like that?

A. That's nice for lunch.

C. Delicious.

B. Well?

D. Food.

B. What kind of food did you have? Ask him if he had soup for dinner, and then fish. Come, now. Admit you had soup for dinner. And a little fish perhaps. Or did you have hors d'oeuvres instead of soup? And steak garni and a sweet, perhaps, or cheese. Did you have cheese? Did you have white wine and red wine and brandy to follow and coffee in little cups? Tell us what you had for dinner.

A. I'm hungry.

B. I'm a bit peckish myself. Never mind that, though. Tell us what you had.

D. Food.

B. For God's sake. He's an idiot. Can you not say anything but food, food, food? If you're hungry you have food. Everybody does. It's a universal custom. But some people like this, some people like that. I'm rather partial to fried food myself, fried bacon, fried sausages, fried egg, fried potatoes. Very nice.

A. Shall I ask him some more questions?

B. I suppose so. Ask him.

A. Are you married.

D. Married.

A. He's married.

D. I am not married.

A. He's a bachelor.

D. I am not a bachelor.

B. Listen. All unmarried men are bachelors. That's true.
It's something to hold on to. All non-bachelors are
either not men or married. True again.

A. It's very peculiar.

B. It's worse than peculiar, it's perverse. I put it to you,
either it's perverse or it's ridiculous. Will you answer
that?

D. I am not married.

B. I take you to assert, I take you to assert that there is
no female creature to whom you stand in a certain
legal relationship known as matrimony.

D. You are correct.

B. Excellent. Therefore you are a bachelor.

D. The category... There is only...

B. Only?

D. Hunger. Need. Sex. Food. Thirst. Drink.

B. Ah!

A. I don't understand.

B. This witness may leave the stand. Your desires are
innocent. Do you hear that? Accused! Stand in the
dock. Your desires are innocent. The blind needs, the
little animals. They are not to blame.

A. They don't know what they're doing?

B. Not that. Not that. They have no thought. They do not particularise. They have no content . They simply desire. You have tastes. They are desires.

D. Desires.

B. Tastes, you see, are your tastes. Desires are human, you see. Lust, jealousy, delicacy, partiality, these belong to you. Whoever is to blame it's not them. That's a fact.

C. Fried onions!

(Pause)

B. What?

C. Fried onions!

B. Fried onions?

C. Yes. You know. Before. (Indignantly) When you were saying you liked fried food. You said you liked fried liver, fried bacon, fried eggs, fried potatoes, but you didn't mention fried onions.

B. So what? Why should I mention fried onions?

C. Well, it just seemed funny, that's all. Missing it out. (Pause. Desperately) I mean, somebody liking fried food would be bound to like fried onions. Wouldn't they? But you missed them out.

B. Well?

C. Well, I was just wondering why you missed them out.

(Pause)

B. Let's get on.

C. Am I to understand that the accused... ?

120

B. Is still accused. That is established.

C. May I, your lordship, may I call the accused?

B. By all means. Call the accused. Accused; you are to answer your defence.

C. M'lud. Have I your lordship's permission to address the court?

B. You have the permission of the court.

C. I thank your lordship. M'lud, you will, of course, be well aware of the seriousness of the charge facing my client. More than anyone, your lordship is aware of the extreme gravity of the offence. This is no simple charge of assault, no mere case of murder or rape, no primitive and inarticulate grasping, some dark night, of an old lady's handbag. Not even, your lordship, a case of an assault on the property of others. No, we are not here to examine such foolish or heated deviations from the paths of righteousness, so clearly and firmly marked out by the law. We live in troubled times, your lordship. Now, it seems, the simple pieties, the natural relations between man and man, man and God, are ignored, not regarded, put to one side. Master and servant, owner and worker, upper and lower, greater and smaller, better and worse, all these, ordained since time began for the preservation of order and the good of man, exist now, where they exist at all, in a state of utter confusion. We cannot, any longer, trust our mouths to speak the right words, our bodies to behave in the correct manner. Brother fails to recognise brother, son his father; man and woman live in a luxury of uninhibited self-indulgence. Here, if anywhere, in a court of law, we must expect order and the just division of man and man to receive their full recognition. I should, your lordship, be failing in my duty if I did not acknowledge, to this court, the extreme gravity of the offence. Nowadays, when crime is sickness, murder a compulsive act, when the fruits of labour are labelled the spoils of war, here at least, everything is as it should be. My client, I know, would rather be found guilty a thousand times,

121

than that the laws should live in disrepute. We do not ask for mercy. We ask for justice.

D. Justice.

B. As you say, Justice. Counsel is to be congratulated upon the beauty of his sentiments.

(Pause)

B. (To C.) You're right.

C. Right?

B. Now I come to think about it, it was funny to miss out fried onions.

C. Oh!

B. Anybody who liked fried food would be bound to like fried onions, you would think.

C. That's what I said.

B. But I missed them out.

C. Yes. That's what set me wondering.

B. It would. It would. Funny. Yes.

(Pause)

B. You missed out fried sausages.

C. I did?

B. You did. Was it deliberate? After all, if I liked the others, as well as fried onions, I'd not be opposed to fried sausages, would I?

C. I suppose not.

B. Well then. Was it deliberate? Did you miss them out on purpose? The sausages.

C. No. I didn't miss them out on purpose. Why should you suppose that?

B. Well (Exasperated) because if I liked the others I'd be sure to like fried sausages and you missed them out. What for?

C. Not for anything. I just forgot, that's all.

B. (Triumphantly) You forgot.

C. (Uneasily) Yes!

B. Well then. That's why I missed out the fried onions.

C. You forgot?

B. Yes. I must have.

C. I see.

   (Pause)

B. Let's get on.

C. I thank your lordship. M'lud: what is the offence of which my client is accused? Broadly speaking, m'lud, and so as not to confuse the court with details, my client is accused, not of an action, precisely, but of a state of being. By being as he is, your lordship, my client has, no less, created disharmony within our community, exacerbated human relations, brought into conflict those who meant only well by each other. By being as he is, it is alleged, my client has created suspicion and hostility where no hostility or suspicion was. Does my client deny this?

B. Does he, does he? Do you deny it?

A. I...

C. He does not. He admits it, your lordship. He and he alone is and was the cause of this late lamented condition of communal strife. Where trust dies, a state of nature returns; each man for himself, no longer the civilized competition of an enlightened self-interest but the wilful hostility of each against each. He admits it, your lordship. He and he alone is the cause. What more then, you will ask, remains but to sentence my client and send him to some place, there to reap the rewards of his wickedness.

B. What more indeed. Prisoner...

C. Your lordship. Your lordship. Let us not be hasty. Justice must not only be done but be seen to be done. Although, as I have said, my client is the cause, the question remains, is he responsible? The madman, the child and atheist all stand in God's eye as innocent. The madman because he is mad, the child because he lacks understanding, the atheist because of his invincible ignorance. My friend, alas, is neither a madman, nor a child, nor, I hope and believe, is he an atheist. No, m'lud, what stands before you, is man himself, free, knowing and culpable. When his hand strikes, it is not the jerk of madness or the foolishness of the child. No, there stands anger, rage, indignation, fear.

B. Fear?

C. Fear.

D. Fear.

A. Wait.

C. I beg your pardon.

A. I said wait.

B. This is not proper. This is not customary. It is neither customary nor proper to stop the defence in the full tide of his eloquence.

A. Things have taken a queer turn.

D. No doubt, no doubt. Things have taken an odd turn.

124

B. May the court be permitted to ask, taking into account that you are the accused and all that, what things and why things have taken a queer turn, or an odd turn?

C. I could certainly do with enlightenment on that point. I could indeed. I was undoubtedly on the verge of a peroration, I could feel it; I knew it was coming on.

A. There will be revelations. It is better to stop now. If we do not stop now there will be revelations.

D. You speak of revelations. Have you anything to confess? Is there anything that in the night, in the dark, in silence, when you are alone, that you say then, that you will say now, anything dreadful, that seems prodigious, too large, too private, too close and queer and particular, that you whisper then, that must not be said, that must not be known, that now you feel the need, the desire, the urge to say. Some things are better not said, some things are true and exist which cannot be true, cannot exist. It destroys the purity of the image, it is like reason that smiles suddenly like a lunatic, something aberrant, outside, something cracking through the thin shell of what is known, described, understood, explained. It is better not to speak.

A. I will not say anything.

D. Ah, but is it not beautiful, is it not pleasant, is it not nice, to speak, to unburden your spirit, to ease yourself? Nothing that is spoken, nothing that is audible or visible, is evil, terrible. Only when shut in the darkness, prowling about in your mind. Confess! Ease yourself. Speak.

A. I will not say anything.

D. Whom you hate, whom you love... Is there no one?

A. I don't hate anyone.

D. But listen, don't you feel it, the anger, black, dirt in your mouth, the hate, don't you feel it?

125

A. Feel it.

D. The hate. Haven't they hurt you, haven't they despised
   you? They won't listen, they won't pay attention.
   There's no respect. You hate them; haven't you felt
   your hands, your strong, white hands slipping around
   their necks, squeezing, yes, the bubbles breaking onto
   their blue lips? Can't you see it? Can't you feel it?
   Yes.

A. (Fascinated, staring) Yes. (In a whisper)

D. Yes, you can see it. You can feel it. The rope, the
   whip, the garrotte, the fire, the nails biting into their
   soft, wet palms. Nice, nice. Can you see it? Can you?

A. Yes, I see it. I see it.

D. And the roar of the music, the music, loud, strong,
   swelling in your ears, the world shaking, the world
   toppling, the buildings rising and walking and crashing.
   The stones cascading in the air. Beautiful.

A. Beautiful.

B. Beautiful.

D. The earth rising to meet you, the planes shrieking.
   Hear them, shrieking, the ground opening like a
   flower, a crimson rose, a steeple of fire. Beautiful.

A. Yes.

D. Don't you want it, don't you need it, the music, the
   fear, the endless, endless destruction?

A. Beautiful.

D. Death, utter stillness. You are yourself. You remain
   yourself, you have demonstrated yourself. No one
   lives as they like. They must submit, yield, give
   themselves, bodies, eyes, appealing, desiring to be
   crushed.

A. Ah.

D. It is yours, isn't it, yours to possess, yours to own. Isn't it? No one must dispossess you, no one must come and take it away.

A. Nobody, nobody. Mine, mine, mine.

D. Who threatens must be destroyed.

A. I demand it. Who threatens must be destroyed.

D. Force must meet force.

A. I demand it. Force must meet force.

D. Men define themselves by their opposition to others.

A. I demand it. I demand it.

D. Freedom is action. Action is assertion. Assertion is power. Power is order. Order is everything.

A. Everything. I, I, I demand it.

D. (Raising his arms) Judgement!

C. Judgement!

B. (Rising and lifting up his arms. He is trembling) Judgement!

   (A. lifts his arms. They all turn towards him. End of scene.)

   (Scene as before, chair still on the table. B. is sitting beside the table. A. is lying with his back to B.)

B. Would you like me to do you an orange? (Silence) It wouldn't be any trouble. (Silence) They're seedless. They're the sort you like. (Silence) Would you like a nut? I'll get the nuts. (Silence) It's good tonight. There's a good programme on. Should I switch it on? Should I? (No answer) Well, blast it! Blast you! I've

explained, haven't I? I got carried away. We all got
carried away. It wasn't very nice for me, I assure you.
Nobody likes to get carried away like that. I've
explained it to you. The least you could do would be to
meet me halfway. (Silence) What do you want me to
do? Go down on my knees? Is that what you want?
Should I go down on my knees? Do you want me to crawl
about on all fours? Shall I bang my head on the floor?
(Silence) Alright then. I'm going down on my knees.
He gets down on his knees) Look, blast you! The least
thing you can do is to look. Look! I'm on my knees.
I'm crawling about on the floor. (He crawls up to the
bed) Look, I'm beating my head on the floor. (He
looks into A. 's face which is without expression) Wuff.
(Seriously, looking into A. 's face) You looked flushed.
You don't look well. Shall I take your temperature?
(A. turns over and faces the other way) I'm going to
get the thermometer. (He walks over to the cupboard)
I'm getting the thermometer. (To himself) It's the
strain. I'd have a temperature if I'd gone through that.
Where's the bloody thermometer? Cheese? Soap?
Bootlaces? Where the hell is the thermometer? This
cupboard should be cleaned up. We'll get everything
organised, everything in the right place. (He turns to
A.) That's what we'll do, eh? You'll just have to say
'thermometer' and I'll say 'right' and go straight to
the cupboard and put my hand on it. (He puts his hand
into the cupboard) Ah, thermometer! (He looks at it,
shakes it down and puts it into his mouth. Mumbles)
We'll both have a check. I say, we'll both have a check.
(Silence. He takes it out and looks at it) Ninety five!
I'm dead. (He staggers about) I'm took. Gorn. Finished. I can feel it. Legs, cold. Belly, cold. Creeping
paralysis. I give and bequeath. (Silence) Alright.
You're sick. Here, put this into your mouth. (He
looks at A. He goes over to him) Under your tongue.
You keep it in for four minutes.

A. It's not sterilised.

B. Oh, indeed. Not sterilised? Very nice. And what do
you think is wrong with me? Eh? Do you think I'm
diseased? Look! I'm as well as I can be.

(He does a few hops around the room)

A.   Elementary hygiene. Nobody knows.

B.   Alright, alright. I'm sterilising it. Look. I'm turning
     on the tap; I'm running the water. I'm sterilising the
     thermometer. (He wipes the thermometer on the seat
     of his trousers) All sterilised. Here. (He puts it into
     A.'s mouth) How's your pulse. (He takes up A.'s hand
     and feels for his pulse) Where's your pulse? You must
     have one. It must be there somewhere. Steady, slow
     drumbeat. Rhythm of life. Where the bloody hell is it?
     You're hiding it from me. Aren't you? Ah, got it. I'll
     count it for fifteen seconds and then multiply by four,
     thus giving us the rate for the minute. 1, 2, 3, 4, 5, 6,
     7, 8, 9, 10, 11, 12, 13, 14, 15, 16, 17, 18, 19, 20, 21,
     22, (Crescendo) 23, 24. Ninety-six. That's fast.
     Definitely fast. Too fast for my liking. You're quiet.
     You're not excited. You're lying on a bed. It's too fast.
     Let's have a look at that temperature. (He takes out
     the thermometer, examines it carefully) A hundred.
     Just as I thought. You're not well.

A.   A hundred. That's bad.

B.   Not too bad. It goes up at night, you see. Just a slight
     fever.

A.   It's not normal.

B.   No, it's not normal. But equally, it's not serious. Just
     a slight fever.

A.   It could be the beginning of something bad.

B.   That's so. It can't be ruled out. It's a possibility to be
     borne in mind, certainly.

A.   I ought to have something. I ought to take something. I
     need treatment. I feel awful.

B.   Do you? Do you really feel awful?

     (Door opens. C. and D. enter)

B. What do you two want? Haven't you caused enough trouble between you? Look at my friend. He's ill. He's definitely not well.

C. I'm genuinely sorry to hear that. What's wrong with him?

B. He's feverish. His temperature is up to a hundred degrees and his pulse is hammering away for dear life.

D. He looks flushed.

B. Of course he does. I've just said he's feverish. He's got a temperature. He needs peace and quiet.

D. He needs treatment.

(D. goes over to A. He bends over and begins to unfasten A.'s shirt)

Put out your tongue. Have you got a sore throat?

A. What's he doing?

B. What are you doing?

C. Let him be, please. My friend has had medical training.

B. You mean he's a doctor. Is that what he is?

C. Well. He's not a doctor, certainly. But he's had medical training. He knows what to look for.

B. Well, that's something. (To A.) That's something, isn't it? If he's had medical training. It's as well to get expert advice. Do you see that?

(D. carries on. He taps A.'s chest and listens. A. puts out his tongue. B. goes over the looks)

B. That's a horrible tongue. It's yellow and green. What have you been doing with your tongue?

D. I don't like it.

B. Do you hear that? Is it serious? Can you say what it is?

A. I feel awful. I feel weak. There's no feeling in my legs. I'm shaking.

C. Look at him. Shaking. That's awful.

D. It's serious.

B. What's he got? Is it infectious? Will we all get it? Oh, this is terrible.

D. It's hardly a physical matter. In that sense. Neurological, I should say. Neurological.

B. Having to do with neurons. Quite so. So it's not infectious?

D. Not exactly. Not exactly infectious.

B. Could you be more precise, doctor. I mean, we all stand in some peril here. We have a right to know. We have ourselves to think of.

C. Exactly, exactly. Much as we feel for the unfortunate patient. We have ourselves to think of.

D. One can't be sure. Infectious? It's hard to say. Is that the right word?

B. Could you put a name to it? It's nice to know what we're all facing.

C. Do we have to be sterilised?

D. Sterilised?

B. Immunised, you mean. Do we have to have injections?

D. No injections. No. Definitely no injections.

B. Could you put a name to it? Does it have a name,
    what he's got?

A. What have I got? Am I done for? I feel I'm going.

    (Excitement. B. and C. crowd round the bed, then
    draw back)

B. He's going, doctor. Can you not do something?

D. It's very difficult. A difficult case. Very difficult.

B. Nobody supposed it would be easy, not with him. If it's
    to do with him it's not easy. Did I ever tell you,
    doctor, he's wilful, there's no doubt about that. He's
    always been wilful.

C. Is there a known treatment?

D. Well!

    (B., C., D. go over to a corner of the room. They
    whisper to each other. D. is earnest and worried but
    forceful. B. is excited and amazed. C. is eager and
    sycophantic to first B. and then D. As they talk B.
    points to the contraption in some surprise. D. appears
    to be questioning him. Occasionally one hears words
    like, electrical, discharge, nodes. All this while A.
    is looking from one to the other and trying to hear what
    they say, to attract attention and generally feeling and
    looking extremely sorry for himself.)

A. What are they talking about? Why don't they talk to me?
    What are they doing over there, all huddled up together?
    What are they whispering? They don't want me to hear.
    I ought to know. I have a right to know. Look at them.
    Huddled up together. I'm the one that's ill. They won't
    tell me. Why don't they tell me? If only I knew what it
    was. If only they would give it a name. Is it shameful
    or something? It must have a name. It must be called
    something. It would be alright, not so bad, I mean, if
    I knew what it was, what they called it. Nodes. I heard
    that. Nodes. What's a node? A point of meeting. A
    crux. What are they talking about nodes for? Electric-

al. What's that got to do with it? I'm cold. Nobody cares a blind bugger. I'm cold. The grave's a cold and solemn place. All those wet worms. Perhaps it's fatal. They're not telling me because it's fatal. They should though. I can face it. I'd rather know. They're treating me like an object. Oh, I don't like it. I'm not happy. I'm anxious. I'm afraid. I'm worried. It's worse when you're treated like an object. I want to die with dignity. I want to choose how to behave. If I know, I'll choose how to behave.

B. It must be done.

(The group breaks up and comes round the bed. They stand silent, looking at A.)

A. Who are you? What do you want?

B. Don't you recognise me? (To D.) He doesn't recognise me.

A. Who are you? Why don't you answer me? (He looks at D.) I know you. I've met you before. We've met before, haven't we? Of course, you're disguised, but I see through you. I know we've met before. (To B.) What's he doing here? Who said he was to be admitted. I gave definite orders he was not to be admitted.

C. Dear me. Dear me. (Whispers to B.) His mind's going.

A. I heard that. (To C.) I know you as well. Little shadow. Wherever he goes he casts your shadow. Echo. Charlatan. Shadow. Nothing. (To B.) He's nothing. Can't you see that? Nothing at all. Can't you see through him?

B. Don't excite yourself, old friend. Don't be excited. Try to keep calm. We're here to help you.

A. Help. You. Who are you? Where do you live? What's your name? Have you got a name? (Silence) You shake your head. You've got no name! Poor little man, no name, nobody knows him.

133

B. Alright, alright. What's <u>your</u> name?

A. Ah, ah. Wouldn't you like to know? I'm not going to tell them. Oh no. (He points to C. and D.) Bend down. I'll tell you. Bend down.

B. (To D.) Is it safe? He might attack me. He might go for my eyes.

D. No danger like that. No danger at all.

B. So you say. So you say. I don't notice you bending down.

D. He doesn't want that.

B. That's true. It's his old friend he wants to talk to. His friend. That's understandable. (Adopting a waggish tone) Well, old friend. Let's hear it, then. Are you going to tell your old friend?

(He bends down. A. whispers. B. jumps back)

B. What do you mean? What are you insinuating? That's horrible. It's not true. You made it up.

C. What did he say?

A. Don't tell him. It's a secret. Don't tell him. I don't want him to know.

B. It was nothing, nothing at all. Just a joke. Wasn't it? A joke.

A. I'll tell you something. It was no joke. It wasn't a joke. Listen.

B. What now?

A. Listen. Armies of them. Whole legions of them. Tramp, tramp, tramp.

C. What's he on about now?

D. Typical. Typical.

134

A. Armies of them. Little grey beings in bowler hats, dusty, like beetles, with bowler hats and umbrellas because of the rain. Deadly.

B. He's off. It's happened. He's gone. Possessed. It's not him any more. I don't recognise him.

A. I don't recognise you. No, I don't. Can't you understand? The rain. Like acid. Bowler hats and umbrellas against a storm of acid. It's a joke. You said so. It's funny.

(He laughs)

B. My God!

A. Do you think it's only me speaking? Do you? Old friend. Me? Your old friend? Friend. It's only me. (He rises from the bed and goes over to B. B. draws away.) Your old friend. Listen, old friend. Do you think it's only me? Eh? Old friend.

B. You're not well. You're not yourself. Lie down, old friend. Lie down now. You've got to keep quiet. You're not well.

A. I'm not well. (He looks stricken for a moment) Not well. (He shakes his head) Who says I'm not well? (He points to D.) Him? Does he say it?

B. We all say it. Don't we? We all say it.

C. & D. We all say it.

A. You're all wrong, then. You're mad. You don't know what you're saying. Listen. I wish to inform you of something. I have something to say. (He climbs up on to the table and stands above them) I'm higher than you are. From where I stand you are of no account whatsoever. Yet I condescend to speak to you. That's nobility. '

B. Come down. You'll fall. You'll hurt yourself. (To D.) Shouldn't we get him down? He shouldn't be climbing

135

about the furniture in that state.

D. Let him be. He'll exhaust himself, then...

A. Listen. I take my chair. I sit in it. I speak.

C. He ought to come down. He's got no business up there. Come down.

A. Silence. Hear what I have to say. Friends and others. I have just received a message from an unimpeachable source. If you tried to impeach this source, if you tried, no matter how hard you tried to impeach him, it, whatever, whoever, you couldn't. It would be silly, absurd, lunatic, ridiculous, beside the point. (He looks round) Beside the point. Listen. What I have to say is that it's all, it's all...

B. All what?

A. All rubbish. Garbage. Stinking refuse. Stench. Horrible. The whiff of it. The stench. It's senseless. Bare conjunction. One damned thing after another. Ah yes. There is no thread. The thread that's wound through the cave of your acts leads to the minotaur. You think. Of your own thoughts. The bloody red-jawed ravening beast. All ravelled. A thousand threads leading to the same bloody, slavering beast. The red mouth, as hot as hell. Backwards, out of the light. Mad. Idiotic, insane. Silence.

(He sinks back into the chair. Talks to himself. B., C., D. edge nearer and nearer)

When the minotaur lived in the air he had a mild face and a beaming eye. A very perfect gentle beast. He collected flowers and classified them. And when the moon came up, he cried. But when he went into the cave, when he went into the cave -

(He looks at D., C., B. who freeze. Then take a step or two back)

Listen. Listen now. When he went into the cave...

136

This is not nice, and he had to buy bread, and the air was foul and it had to be pumped down to him; they covered his legs and his arms with chains, they loaded him down with chains and he started to roar. The cave resounded to his howls, the cave shook to the roars of the chained minotaur. Howling, howling. Morning, noon and night. Hideous with his noise. Poor beast.

D. Now.

(They leap on him and hold him down in his chair. He looks from one to the other)

A. What are you doing? What's this for? Let me alone. What are you doing?

B. It's nothing. You're not well.

A. Am I not? Is that it? Can't I go to bed?

C. Just you be quiet now. Just relax. Don't tremble so much. Relax. Try not to shake so much.

A. I am shaking. I remember. (To B.) Do you remember? We found out about it. This shaking.

B. Yes, yes.

(D. is beside B.'s contraption. He draws up belts with clasps and shows them to B.)

D. Are these the straps?

B. Straps? I suppose so.

D. They'll do very well. Excellent

A. What are the straps for?

B. Never mind, never mind.

A. What are the straps for?

D. Round here.

(He climbs up behind A. who struggles to see what he's doing. He draws a strap around A.'s arms and clicks it shut at the back)

A. What's this. This isn't nice. What's this for? Let me alone. Leave me alone. (To B.) Tell them to leave me alone.

D. The legs.

(He straps the legs in the same way)

D. That ought to hold him.

B. Are you sure we're doing the right thing? Are you sure you know what you're doing?

C. Trust my friend. He knows what he's doing.

D. These are the nodes, I suppose. Yes. That's right. One here.

(Clamps node to A.'s head. Wire trails to the contraption. A. looks wildly from one to the other.

A. Don't let him do that. Why do you let him do that? Where's his authority? Who put him in charge? Did we vote for it? (To B.) Did we have a vote? Was it a duly democratic procedure? Have I forgotten something?

B. No, no. Be quiet now. Do what he says. Don't get excited. Try and be calm. It's for the best. Isn't it?

D. Now one on each wrist. So. Good. Very good.

C. How do you operate it?

B. Well, it's not finished, you know. There a lot of theory yet. It's not exactly predictable. There's an element, an established degree of probability. Nothing's certain. It's experimental. It needs more thought.

C. How do you operate it? How does it go?

B. Well. You see the little box, with the button on the top. You press the little button, you see. That makes the contact and then the power is boosted through the transformers and it should go.

D. Is it earthed?

B. Well, now you have it. Those three terminals there. Those three. They have to be fixed to earth it. It should be internally earthed. But it was difficult, you see, fiddling. Not without hazard. Some risk.

D. It can be done. Here. (He turns to C.) You hold that.

C. Is it alright?

D. Perfectly safe.

B. An element of risk. Slight. To be discounted.

D. (To B.) Take this, will you?

B. Er, well. As I said...

D. Here you are. (Places it in B.'s hand) Now I hold this one.

C. His teeth have begun to chatter.

D. Mmm. One moment. A slight adjustment.

(He produces a short strap which he slips under A.'s jaws and fastens at the top of his head. Just before he does this A. says -)

A. Don't do...

D. Well, that's all very satisfactory. It only remains to press the button and we've done it.

B. Who presses the button, then? Let me say from the outset that I will not, under any circumstance, take it upon myself to do so.

C. It's your contraption. You made it. You know what it's for. It's your responsibility.

B. It's out of my hands.

C. That's all very well. But I certainly can't press it. I don't know one end of a contraption from another. I'm prepared to play my part, and after all, it's really got nothing to do with me. I was drawn in, you might say, against my better judgment. As you well know, I keep myself to myself. I've never tried to cause trouble. (He nods at A.) He'd tell you that, if he could speak, wouldn't you? (A.'s eyes turn and stare at him) Well, it's true. I am the injured party here. I don't see why I should take the responsibility.

B. Oh, very good, very good. The first rat to desert the sinking ship. There he is.

(Points to A.)

B. My friend. You've known him, how long? Years. Years. Always ready to do you a good turn, wasn't he? And haven't I always been a good friend of yours? Have I ever troubled you? We've always got on. Well, I must say, it takes a situation like this to show who your true friends are.

D. Gentlemen. There is no need to quarrel. Obviously it's neither your duty, (To B.) nor yours, (To C.) to bring this to its appropriate conclusion. Nor mine. Nor mine, gentlemen. Gentlemen. What are you thinking of? Do you not realise where the duty lies, whose responsibility it must be? Look no further, gentlemen. Behold, the man. (He points to A.)

B. What, him? You mean him?

D. Of course. How shall we take it upon ourselves to determine his action? He is free, gentlemen, free. Let him, out of his freedom, choose for himself. Gentlemen. It is an act of expiation. We know where the responsibility lies. Let him shoulder that responsibility. Let him act for himself.

C. Do it himself, you mean? Him? He'll never do it. He'll never manage it.

D. Do not say that. Who can imagine what strength, what power, what courage lurks behind those trembling lips, that sweating skin? Make no mistake, gentlemen, he will rise to it, he will assert himself. You will be surprised, gentlemen, he will surprise you. Accepting his burden, shouldering his responsibility, trembling, perhaps, afraid, he will rise to the occasion. Make no mistake about that.

B. That's right, that's right. (Turning to A.) Do you hear him praising you? Can you hear what he's saying up there? Don't you feel proud? Don't you feel uplifted?

D. Gentlemen. There is a brave man. Salute him gentlemen. Honour where honour is due. Let us show, gentlemen, once and for all, our respect, nay, our reverence, our humility, in the face of such dignity, such courage.

(As he says this A.'s eyes grow wild. He stares from one to the other like an animal. He strains at the straps. He is heard trying to speak. They stand before him and raise their arms in salute)

D. To work, to work. Bring over the box. (C. goes over to get the box. Carries it carefully, at arms length, towards the table. He stumbles. Almost drops it. There is a yelp of alarm from B.)

B. You crazy lunatic. Do you not see us holding these wires. If you'd dropped that there's no knowing what would have happened.

C. You take it, then. I'm shaking. My hands are all wet. I can't hold it.

B. I'm no better.

D. Gently, gently. Raise his legs, gentlemen. Give me the box. (He fits the box under A.'s feet) You understand, don't you? You press the button, the little button, you

141

press the button resting under your feet. Press it gently but firmly. You understand.

(A. stares at him. Pause. Then he slowly, very slowly, bows his head)

D. Back, gentlemen, back.

B. Wait. Wait. The wires, the wires. Fools.

(Both B. and C. are terror-stricken and cannot loose their hold on the wires)

D. (Dropping his wire) NOW.

(A. stamps with his foot. B. and C. give a loud cry. There is a crack and a flash. They are seen, all of them, illuminated in the glare. Then B. and C. fall. A. shivers and slumps, hanging in the straps. As this is happening, books, clothes, chairs, bed, shake and collapse; the door falls forward. There is a rush of wind into the room, rising to a crescendo and dying away. D. is standing, all this while, smiling. He steps forward, takes off his spectacles and surveys the scene. He speaks quietly, affectionately, facing the audience)

D. It is over. It is finished. It is done. I grant them, I grant you, the courtesy of an epilogue. (He turns and touches C. with his foot) There he is, a small man, in brown shoes, blue socks and a green tie. A body with clothing. (Moves over to B.) I pick my way delicately from one to the other. And there he is. Ingenious, inventive, quick-witted, overweening, affectionate. Dead. (Pause) Not a word. (He points to A.) And there he is. Troubled, capable of profundity, absurd, farcical, blameworthy, not to blame. I close my eyes, ladies and gentlemen, and nobody sees. Everybody is blind. I close my eyes.

(He stands smiling, his eyes closed)

(The curtain closes.)

OTHER C AND B PLAYSCRIPTS

                            * Hardcover + Paperback

* All plays marked thus are represented for Dramatic
presentation by C and B (Theatre) Ltd, 18 Brewer Street ,
London W1

GAMBIT

INTERNATIONAL THEATRE REVIEW

Calder and Boyars also publish a quarterly theatrical review, GAMBIT. This exciting and informative magazine was first established in order to bring new plays to a wider audience, intending to bridge the gap between the number of good new plays being written and the number of these plays which are staged in important theatres.

Each issue contains the text of at least one full-length play as well as an editorial, articles on current trends in the theatre and coverage of new plays and productions throughout the world.

Past contributors to the magazine have included Jean-Paul Sartre, Eugene Ionesco, Jack McGowran, David Tutaev, Paolo Levi, Fernando Arrabal and Max Frisch.

Recent Editions
GAMBIT 15- Swiss Theatre, including the play THE CAT by Otto F. Walter and articles by Lydia Benz-Burger and Victor Corti.

GAMBIT 16- Fringe Theatre, including plays by John Grillo, A. F. Cotterell and Jeff Nuttall.

GAMBIT 17- will be devoted to an assessment of the plays of Edward Bond and will contain a long discussion between the author, Harold Hobson, Irving Wardle, Jane Howells, John Calder and Marion Boyars about his work.

Subscription rates: STERLING 6 issues £2.15.0. or 4 issues £1.17.6 post free: U.S.A. and CANADA 6 issues $8.50 or 4 issues $6.25, post free. Price per issue 10s. 6d. or $1.75, postage 2s. or 30 cents.